Other Books by Kate L. Mary

The Broken World Series:
Broken World
Shattered World
Mad World
Lost World
New World
Forgotten World
Silent World
Broken Stories

The Twisted Series:
Twisted World
Twisted Mind
Twisted Memories
Twisted Fate

The Oklahoma Wastelands
The Loudest Silence

Zombie Apocalypse Love Story Novellas:
More than Survival
Fighting to Forget
Playing the Odds
Key to Survival
Surviving the Storm
The Things We Cannot Change

The Blood Will Dry

Collision

The College of Charleston Series:
The List
No Regrets
Moving On
Letting Go

When We Were Human

Alone: A Zombie Novel

The Moonchild Series:
Moonchild
Liberation

Anthologies:
Prep For Doom
Gone with the Dead

For Rebekah, who suggested I watch *The 100*,
which helped inspire this world.
You were right. It's amazing

OUTLIERS

KATE L. MARY

Twisted Press

Published by Twisted Press, LLC, an independently owned company.

Cover Art by Kate L. Mary
Edited by Proof Corrections by Callie

ONE

T HE FEAST WAS THE BIGGEST ONE YET. AFTER THREE years of working in the House of Saffron, I should have been used to it. But there were days when no matter what I did, I found it impossible to block out the sights and smells that accompanied my job. The smoky fragrance of roasted meat that begged my stomach to pay it mind, and the mountain of mashed potatoes, complete with rivers of melted butter carving their way through the peaks. No matter how hard I tried to ignore it all, there were moments when my senses took over. On those days my arms and legs worked on muscle memory alone. Carrying the bottle of wine, pouring it ever so carefully so as not to ruin the fine clothes of the people sitting around the table. Serving the dessert, baked apples with cinnamon or raspberries sprinkled with chocolate, all things that never once in my twenty-four years of life had passed my lips. Things that made my mouth water and my knees threaten to give out. Things that my stomach begged for.

Today was one of those days.

It was to be expected. Yesterday had been a bad day, so I had taken my meager rations from the kitchen home to Anja and our mother. It was something that the head housemaid frowned upon, but as long as I only did it sparingly, she chose to look the other way.

"Indra."

The sound of my name cutting through the conversation snapped my brain into focus. Saffron was at the head of the table, sitting with her back so straight that it looked as if she had a board tied to it, and she was waving me over.

"Mistress." I bowed when I stopped at her side, careful to keep my head down.

She was a short woman, as were all the Sovereign, and standing with my head dipped the way it was meant that we were practically eye to eye. This close up her skin appeared fake. It was the same pale shade as everyone who lived in the city, but waxy and much too smooth to belong to a woman more than half a century old. Her cold eyes were the same shade of gray as her hair, and she possessed a healthy roundness that signified her station in life, yet did not boast the same gluttony most of the other Sovereign's bodies did. Standing next to her always made me feel like a withered leaf that would soon be blown away by the wind, and today was no different.

"Your master just had the most wonderful thought," Saffron paused the way she always did when she spoke. It was her way of making sure everyone was paying attention, something she should have been unconcerned about within these walls. When the head of this house spoke, it felt like the whole world was holding its breath. "Do you know of someone in need of a job?"

I kept my head low, but my eyes snapped up faster than usual. Was this a trick? Saffron had no sense of humor, but the request still felt *wrong*. The Sovereign had not created a new position in decades. Our jobs were passed down from generation to generation. Three years ago, when my mother had gotten too sick to keep working, I had taken her place, just as she had taken the place of her mother when she was a young woman.

"A young boy, perhaps?" Saffron continued when I said nothing. "It's just that Lysander is about to become a man and I'm sure he could use a Hand to help him throughout the day. He will be starting his own life very soon, you know."

I did know. Everyone knew that the son of Saffron and Bastian was about to marry. The house had been preparing for the celebration for nearly a year. I was also painfully aware of the fact that Saffron's only child had been a man for many years now. A man who preyed on the kitchen staff, who cornered women in the pantry and had his way with them. I had been in that position myself, but only once after first arriving at the house. After that I had learned how to watch my back, being careful never to make myself vulnerable so I would be forced to endure the humiliation of that day again. Not that my efforts had prevented other women from succumbing to the same fate. It was impossible to recount how many times I had been forced to stand by and do nothing as the pleas of another woman penetrated the pantry door. There was nothing for me to do, of course, but I hated myself all the same. Lysander of Saffron was a monster, and yet he was among the class that ruled our little world, and Outliers like myself were powerless to do anything to stop it.

Saffron's gray eyes held mine as she waited for my response. They were like two stones, as cold and emotionless as she was, and yet sincere. She was being genuine in her inquiry, and even though I found it impossible to understand the motivation behind her sudden goodwill gesture, hope bloomed in my chest. A position like this could change a family's life.

"I do, Mistress," I said, once again lowering my eyes. With Saffron, or any of the Sovereign for that matter, eye contact needed to be kept as brief as possible. "I know the perfect boy for the position."

"He isn't too young, is he?" Bastian asked, and as always I found it difficult not to cringe at the sound of his nasally voice. It was fortunate that he rarely spoke.

Keeping my head bowed, I allowed my gaze to move across the table to Saffron's husband. He was a plump man, even bigger than average, with a gut that strained against his shirt, threatening to pop the little white buttons that kept it closed. Like his wife, Bastian's skin appeared waxy in the light of the kitchen, but that was common for Sovereign since they spent very little time outside.

Bastian dabbed his napkin at his mouth before saying, "We don't need a good-for-nothing running around the house."

"No, Master," I said, once again focusing my eyes on the floor. The rug under me was worn but still bright, and soft under my tired feet. "Ten. The perfect age for training."

"Indra knows our ways. She will pick a good one," Saffron said, dismissing her husband with a slight wave of her hand. "Her family has served us faithfully for centuries." A pause. "How is Dichen?"

I curled my fingers and dug my nails into the fleshy part of my hand. "My mother is very good, Mistress. I will tell her that you asked after her."

"Good, good. It was a shame to lose her, but you have proven to be just as manageable as she was. It's not always the case, you know." Saffron was no longer talking to me. She had turned to the guest at her right hand, the mistress of the neighboring house, but I remained where I was. "Eslanda, you've had such a difficult time with your help, have you not?"

"The most difficult time." Eslanda paused with a fork full of mashed potatoes halfway to her mouth and the electric lights glistened off the butter. "That's why I'm supporting Stateswoman Paizlee's bill."

Saffron frowned at her guest as she waved her fingers at me, motioning that I was dismissed. "You can't be serious."

I backed away as Eslanda raised a plump hand to stop Saffron from saying anything else. The head of the neighboring house was robust, twice as big as Saffron, and the rolled skin at her neck was a bitter reminder of how much those living in the city had compared to my own people.

"I know you've had good fortune with the Outliers in your service," Eslanda said, "but not all of us have been so lucky. One of them stole from the House of Kora only last week." She popped the mound of potatoes into her mouth in a triumphant gesture.

"What's this?" Bastian asked, his nasally voice booming through the room, earning him a glare from his wife. "We haven't had a gathering in years."

"Well, I may be exaggerating." A white speck flew from Eslanda's mouth and landed on the lace tablecloth, lost in the intricate white design just as I turned my back to the table. "But there was an incident at the house. I'm not certain exactly what happened, but whatever it was, it was enough for Kora to change her views on the bill. We need more regulations when it comes to the Outliers. We can't just let them in and out of the city like they're one of us. They aren't. They're *different*."

The last word seemed to hit me in the back, and for the first time today the wobble in my legs had nothing to do with the food piled to excess on the table. My steps faltered as I passed the line of Fortis guards, and the one closest to me reached out when I stumbled. He caught himself before his fingers could make contact with my arm though, and his hand dropped to his side as his fingers curled into a fist.

"Are you okay?" he asked in a voice just loud enough that I was able to discern it above the conversation going on behind me.

Shock forced my gaze up, but the man was so tall that I found it difficult to keep my head down while lifting my eyes to meet his. I had seen him before, every day since first coming to work in the house, but until now he had never addressed me directly. He was older than me, but not by much.

Currently he stood in the shadowy recesses of the room, making his bronzed skin look darker than usual. The light hanging above the dining room table at my back cast a shadow across his face, accentuating his strong features and making his brown eyes look almost black. His hair was cut close to his scalp, so short that he almost appeared bald, and unlike many of his Fortis companions, his face was free of hair.

The man's gaze met mine, but only for a beat before I once again lowered my eyes to the floor. The House of Saffron was one of the most affluent homes in Sovereign City and employed more guards than the average house inside the walls. Still, during my three years of employment, not once had I ever spoken to the dozen or so men and women who guarded the family. The Fortis may not have been Sovereign, but they were still better than me. I was an Outlier. I was nothing.

I nodded once in response to the man's question, not daring to utter a sound, and then hurried to my place among the other Outliers.

Isa stood at my side, and the uniform she wore looked on the verge of swallowing the bony fourteen-year-old girl's body. She had been in the house for only two weeks now, having replaced her sister, Emori, who was too swollen with child to continue working. Unlike most of the Outliers who came to work in the city, Isa had lost weight since she started. I knew why: she had been sneaking her rations to her pregnant sister, but I also knew it would have to stop. Once a week was acceptable, but if Isa took food outside the city too often, even if it had been given to her, someone would take notice and accuse her of stealing, an offense that Outliers rarely risked. The penalty for theft was much too harsh.

Isa tugged at the sleeve of her dress, a sign that she was not yet used to wearing the strange clothes of the Sovereign. It was a sensation I remembered all too well. The fabric of the uniform was too stiff, too unnatural feeling after a lifetime of wearing fur and animal hides. Although it was not the fabric alone that made Outliers feel like intruders in this world. The clothes the Sovereign wore were too colorful, unnaturally bright and garish compared to the drabness of Sovereign City, as well as too long and with too much excess fabric in general. The women wore dresses with sleeves that covered the entire length of their arms, even when it was not cold outside, and skirts that flowed around their legs when they walked. The men, too, seemed to dress more for looks than for comfort, with long pants and clunky shoes, and jackets that were unnecessary for keeping warm. Despite how hard my mother had tried to prepare me for my position in the city, it had still taken me some time to adjust to the new world I had suddenly found myself immersed in, just as I knew it would be for Isa.

I had been much older than her when I arrived at Saffron's house though, and the passage markings on the young girl's temples that indicated she was now the main provider for her household seemed to contrast with the childish roundness of her face and the flatness of her chest. Fourteen was much too young. Even when I had received the passage markings on my own temples at the age of twenty-one, I had felt the weight of the lines. It had not been the pain of the half circles and dots being carved into my skin, but the knowledge that it was up to me to make sure my mother and sister did not starve. I could only imagine how difficult it was for Isa.

"Did you eat the stew you were given this morning?" I whispered to Isa. I had to look up because even at fourteen she was taller than me, which was not unusual. Almost everyone towered over me.

On my other side, Mira shot me a warning look, but I ignored her and focused on the teen.

Isa shook her head.

"You must," I whispered, my gaze darting to the table quickly before going back to the girl. "You have taken Emori enough food."

"She needs it." The teen stuck her chin out defiantly and kept her eyes straight ahead, avoiding my gaze.

"She also needs a sister who has both hands."

Isa's dark eyes shot down, capturing mine. They were big eyes, round and brimming with innocence. The eyes of a child who had been protected too well by her mother and older sister. Emori and Cera had thought they were helping Isa by taking on the burden of life for her, but now that the girl had been forced into service, her naïveté was a hindrance. She needed to be better acquainted with the ways of the city or her time in the House of Saffron would be short, and then Cera, Emori, and the baby that would soon join them, would struggle to survive.

"You promise me you will eat the stew?" I hissed again.

Mira's fingers wrapped around my wrist and I tore my gaze from the young girl at my side so I could focus on the table. Saffron was watching me from across the room, her gray eyes like icy thorns. I would be punished later, I knew, but I also knew that I could not let Isa be found out. Her punishment would be much greater than mine.

"Promise," I hissed, talking out of the corner of my mouth even as I watched Saffron. The mistress's lips turned down, but I was rewarded for my efforts when Isa's head bobbed twice.

I lowered my head and only a beat later Mira's hand slipped from my wrist, but not before I felt the tremble in her arm.

Two

AFTER DINNER, THE FAMILY AND THEIR GUESTS retired to the drawing room while the servants went about the task of clearing the table. We did it wordlessly, knowing that Saffron was still nearby and would not tolerate conversation of any kind while company was in the house. Around the room, the Fortis guards stood watching over us, and the black fabric of their uniforms blended into the shadowy corners as if they would soon become one with the darkness.

The room was silent enough that I was able to discern the quiet hum of electricity from the light hanging above the table. A "chandelier" Saffron called it. It consisted of nearly a dozen light bulbs and hundreds of polished balls of glass dangling around them. I had never seen anything like it before coming to work here, and had been enthralled by the delicate balls for the first few weeks in the house. Then I had been tasked with cleaning the thing. Spending hours on a ladder polishing the little pieces of glass had cured me of the obsession. Now I only saw it as a nuisance.

When the dishes had been cleared, I stripped the lace tablecloth off and took it to the back of the house. The air in the laundry room was cozy and warm, and the drone of the dryer as it flipped the clothes nestled inside was soothing enough to make me wish I could curl up and take a nap the way the Sovereign often did after their midday meal. A silly wish, and one that would never come to fruition for someone like me.

Back in the kitchen, the other Outliers were washing pots and pans, and packing leftover food away. The atmosphere was less tense than it had been in the dining room because we were no longer within earshot of Saffron. The kitchen was the one place in the house where we were able to talk a little more freely, and even though it had its limitations, I was always thankful for the break.

Isa alone was not working, but instead sat at the table in the corner of the room eating her stew, much to my relief. The girl had appeared thin in the dim light of the dining room, but in the brightness of the kitchen it looked as if her collarbones were trying to push their way through her dark skin. She had been giving her sister too much, something I would need to address. Pregnant or not, Emori had to know that Isa needed the food just as much as she did.

"I started the wash," I told the head housemaid, Siri, when I stopped in front of her.

"Good." The older woman made a face when she hefted a pot up off the counter and passed it to me.

Nearing her fiftieth year, she was the oldest Outlier working in the house. She had taken the position when my mother retired three years earlier, and I knew that Siri was not far from retirement herself. The work was taking a toll on her and I could see it in the lines of her face, interwoven with her many passage markings, and the gray streaked through her dark hair. She had put in good time, but I knew that before long she would be forced to pass the position to her own daughter.

I carried the pot over to the sink where Mira was already busy washing one and set it on the counter. "I have another one for you."

She looked my way for only a second before her gaze moved to Isa. "You need to let her make her own mistakes."

I exhaled and took the clean pot to dry while Mira dipped the dirty one into the soapy water.

"How can I do that? If I see her making a mistake, I will do what I can to correct her. To save her from some of the pain of life."

"At your own peril?" Mira kept her eyes on the pot when she said it.

I shrugged, but said nothing in response.

We washed and dried in silence for a moment, Mira focusing on getting every spot off the pot and me staring at the water as I dried. The steam rising off of it never failed to amaze me.

"Indra."

My back stiffened at the sound of Saffron's voice, and next to me Mira froze, allowing the pot to slip from her hands and sink into the soapy water. I refused to look my friend's way when I set the pot in my own hands down, or when I turned to face the mistress.

Saffron was standing just inside the door to the kitchen, the frown on her face pulling her waxy skin tight until it appeared as if the tendons in her neck would break through.

"Mistress." I curtsied, ducking my head down in the process.

"My office. Now."

Saffron spun on her heel and her skirts swished around her as she headed back through the door. I followed obediently, feeling Mira and Isa's gazes on my back as I went. The punishment would not be fun, but it would be worth it knowing that Isa had listened to me.

Saffron had already taken her place behind the ancient mahogany desk by the time I reached her office. I only knew the thing was mahogany because she emphasized it so often. As if any of us knew what mahogany even was, or the difference between how it and oak needed to be cleaned. Not that we dared show our ignorance to the mistress of the house. In situations like these, it was best to keep your mouth shut and nod.

The desk shone under the electric lights, just like the wood floors beneath my feet did. The house was hundreds of years old but wore its age with dignity, as did the furniture and pictures and other random décor, all things that I had never seen before coming to work here. Mirrors imprisoned by intricate frames, pictures that displayed bodies of water that seemed to go on forever, and lights that turned on with the flick of a switch. Everything inside the city was foreign to an Outlier like myself, from the electricity that ran through the city to the clothes the Sovereign wore.

"You were talking during dinner," Saffron said before I had even had a chance to shut the door.

I turned to face her, my head down and my hands clasped in front of me: a perfect picture of submission. "Yes, Mistress."

"I haven't had to chastise you since the first few weeks of your service. That was, what, three years ago?"

"Yes, Mistress," I repeated.

"I expect more from you, Indra. Your mother was head housemaid, and I expected that you would take the position when Siri retires. Have I not treated you well? Have I not put all of my trust in you by allowing you to pick a Hand for Lysander?"

I dug my nails into my palms as I often did when faced with a ridiculous question. As if anyone in the city had ever attempted to treat the Outliers fairly.

"You have done well by me, Mistress," I lied, the words coming out smoothly despite how difficult I found it to push them past my lips.

"Then what, may I ask, was so important that you felt the need to talk during my dinner?"

"Isa," I explained, my eyes still on the ground, "the new girl who took Emori's place."

I ventured a look up at the mention of the maid who had left, curious if Saffron had any clue that the baby growing in her stomach was of her blood. Her grandchild. Wondering if the woman in front of me knew or cared what her son was really like. There was no acknowledgement on the Mistress's face though, and the cold eyes fixed on me were as emotionless as ever.

"Isa needed some more direction and I felt that it could not wait," I continued. "She is young and naïve, and I wanted to be sure she understood the rules so she would not get in trouble." I shook my head slightly when the words came out, then corrected myself by saying, "So she would not break your trust."

Saffron may have been a cold woman, but she was a woman of her word, something she prided herself in. We were all told the same thing upon arriving in her house: if we kept her trust, we would be treated fairly. She was true to that promise. As much as a Sovereign could be, anyway. It made her better to work for than many of the other people living inside these walls, a fact I knew well since I had been loaned out to other houses on multiple occasions to help with celebrations. Saffron had little concern for the people working in her house, but she did care about appearances.

"I know you feel protective of your people and that's an honorable thing, but you must know that by talking during my dinner, you have betrayed my trust. You don't speak unless spoken to, especially when we have company in the house." Saffron let out a long sigh that could have come across as regret were it not for the lack of feeling in her eyes. "You know you'll need to be punished."

"I do, Mistress," I replied.

"It will be as much of an example to Isa as the guidance you gave her earlier was." Saffron's chair scraped against the floor when she stood, and despite my best efforts, my body jerked in response. "Kneel."

I did as I was told, keeping my head down as I sank to my knees in the middle of the office. The wood floor was hard and cold against my knees, even through the thick skirt of my uniform.

"Arms out in front of you," Saffron said as she moved closer, her skirts swishing around her with every step.

I did as I was told, putting my arms out in front of me, palms up, but I kept my eyes down.

"Five."

I closed my eyes even though I knew I would not be able to keep them that way.

"Eyes open, Indra. Head up."

I lifted my chin and forced my lids open. Saffron was right in front of me now, so close that the folds of her skirt almost touched my fingertips. The tendrils of the small whip she used for punishment dangled between us, and the scent of leather tickled my nostrils. The smell was different than the hide we used in our village, and would forever be associated with this woman and this room, with pain and humiliation. The smallest whiff of it made my skin sting, just as it was now.

"Count," Saffron commanded as she raised the whip.

It came down before I had a chance to respond, and the strips stung against my palms, forcing a gasp out of me.

I had to swallow before I could whisper, "One."

The second lash brought tears to my eyes and welts to the palms of my ivory skin. The number "two" came out of my mouth automatically, and the third blow came only a beat later. I gasped out the next number, my voice shaking as much as my arms were. My palms were crisscrossed with red welts, the skin not broken but swollen where the leather had struck me. I cried out with the next strike, the number "four" being forced past my lips with the yelp, and then Saffron brought the whip down for the fifth and final time.

"Five!" It felt as if the glass in the windowpanes shook with the force of my scream, and my cheeks were streaked with tears. Underneath me, my legs wobbled, but somehow I managed to stay on my knees.

I kept my arms out in front of me, knowing that Saffron would want to inspect the welts lining my hands. She would do it under the pretense that she wanted to be certain no medical attention was needed, but I had long suspected that she secretly enjoyed seeing the pain she inflicted on others. Even though she did not beat her servants the way some of the other Sovereign did, I believed there was a part of her that craved the dishing out of pain. I even wondered if she used that whip on Bastian when they were alone in their room at night. It seemed like something she would do.

Saffron bent down so she could get a closer look at my palms. "No skin was broken. You should be fine to return to work."

I kept my arms up when I nodded.

Saffron stared at my hands for a few beats longer, and I ventured a glance up. Her icy gaze was focused on my palms, but for once her eyes were not devoid of emotion. Excitement flickered in them.

I averted my gaze before she noticed me staring, but I knew the expression would stay with me until the day I died.

Saffron turned away and I was finally allowed to lower my arms. I rested them on my knees, palms up. They throbbed, pulsing like every welt had a heartbeat of its own. I wanted to curl my fingers into fists and beat them against the back of Saffron's head, but I could do neither. My palms hurt too much to even consider making a fist, and if I struck a Sovereign I would be put to death. If something happened to me, Anja would have to take my place in Sovereign City and no one would be around to take care of our mother. She was too sick to spend her days alone anymore.

Saffron didn't even glance my way when she said, "You may go."

"Thank you, Mistress," I said.

Getting to my feet without using my hands was difficult, but I managed. I had been in this position before, although it had been nearly three years since my last punishment. Saffron had been right about that, which to me was another sign of how much she savored these moments. Outliers kneeling on the floor of her office, bending to her will more than ever before. It was the only way to explain how she remembered exactly when my last punishment had been. With all the people in her employment and all the punishments she dished out—several a week—it seemed unlikely that she would remember who had been punished and when. Especially when so much time had passed.

Mira rushed to my side the second I set foot in the kitchen. "How many?" Her heart shaped face contorted into an ugly version of itself and her forehead wrinkled, pulling her passage markings together until they formed one continuous line above each eyebrow instead of four dashes.

"Five," I said, allowing my friend to take my hands in hers.

Her palms, like mine, were decorated with callouses, and her knuckles and joints were dry and cracked from washing too many dishes. It was soothing though, having hands that were so familiar on mine. Mira and I had been through a lot together over the years, and she had come to work at Saffron's house only a couple months after I did. Unlike me, however, Mira had earned more than her fair share of punishments. So many, in fact, that if I looked hard enough I could detect the faint lines of the last lashes still decorating the pale skin of her palms.

"Five?" My friend shook her head in disbelief.

"You know that is the minimum."

"I thought she might be merciful with you," Mira murmured. "You are her favorite."

"Favorite?"

She kept her gaze on my palms. Our skin was the same shade, pale but freckled from years of being exposed to the harsh sun. Once summer returned, though, that would change. Mine would tan to a nice golden color while hers would refuse to comply. It had two shades, ivory and pink, and Mira always said she spent the entire summer fighting a battle with the sun, knowing that she would lose no matter what she did.

"You must know that Saffron likes you the best," she said, finally pulling her gaze away from the welts. Her eyes met mine; they were as pale blue as the sky on a clear day, and as pretty as the rest of her was.

"Saffron does not like anyone."

"You are too modest, Indra." Mira released my hands. "We should put ice on these."

"You know we cannot. The freezer is off limits to us." My gaze moved to the small window above the sink. I could see a sliver of sky from where I stood, and it seemed to me that the gray clouds were thicker now than they had been this morning. "Maybe it will snow."

"If we are lucky," Mira replied, and when I looked back, her head was bent.

We both knew that snow would not be a lucky thing for anyone in the village but us.

"I will be fine," I assured her. "But if Saffron catches us standing around instead of working, I will not and neither will you. We need to get back to work."

Mira nodded her assent, and together we retreated to the sink where the dirty dishes sat waiting.

THREE

T HE THROB IN MY HANDS WAS INCESSANT BY THE time Mira and I left Saffron's house to head home, but I tried my best to hide it from my friend. She knew I was only putting on a brave face—she had been here more often and more recently than I had—but she too pretended that the welts lining my palms were nothing.

Outside, the air had a chilly bite to it despite the sun shining down on Sovereign City, telling me it would be nearly impossible to stay warm tonight. Anja, our mother, and I would be forced to huddle together in one bed if we wanted to get any sleep at all, not that I expected to unless the throb in my hands lessened.

Mira wrapped her arms around herself as we walked. "It is going to snow in the wilds."

"It is," I replied.

The skirts of our uniform dresses had been pulled up around our knees and pinned so they would not drag on the ground as we walked, and every time a chilly gust of wind made it into the city, bumps popped up on my legs, making me wish I could leave the skirt down. It was impossible, though. We did not have the resources in our village to wash the dresses, and since Saffron only had it done for us once a week, we did everything in our power to make sure the uniforms stayed clean in between. It was a difficult task, especially once snow fell on the wilds.

"Who are you going to pick to fill the spot?" Mira asked only a short time after we had left the house.

It was a question I had been expecting, and one I knew Mira hated to ask almost as much as I hated to give her my answer.

When Saffron first offered to let me choose someone to work in her house, it had felt like she was handing me a key that would open the gates of prosperity to a family in our village. But as the day wore on, the weight of the decision had begun to settle over me. The responsibility was much bigger than I had first realized. Yes, I was going to be able to give one family a life altering opportunity, but only one. It was not enough, not by far, and I knew that no matter who I chose, someone was going to hate me for the decision.

"You know I cannot pick Kye." I glanced my friend's way out of the corner of my eye, unable to meet her gaze as I waited for her response.

Mira nodded as she rubbed her hands up and down her arms. Her cheeks were pink from the cool air, as was the tip of her nose, and the added color made her look twice as pretty as usual.

"I know."

I stopped and turned to face Mira, forcing her to do the same. All around us people passed, most of them Fortis and other Outliers, but a few Sovereign as well. They were bundled under robes that had thick hoods to protect their skin from the sun, but I was still able to catch the looks they shot us as they walked by. Looks that said we needed to keep moving. I knew they were right, but I wanted to say this one thing while I had the courage. I wanted to make sure Mira understood.

"I wish I could, I really do," I said, looking up at my friend. Like everyone else I knew, she was taller than me. "But you already have a job in the city, and it would be unfair. This would open the gates for a whole family for generations to come, and I feel like I have to pick someone else."

"Indra—" Mira put her hand on my arm, and even through the stiff fabric of my uniform I could feel the chill from her skin. "I know. I understand and so will Kye. I am not going to lie; I wish you could choose him. I wish he could have a job inside the walls too, but I know it would be unfair."

I let out a deep breath and the tension that had begun to gather between my shoulder blades throughout the day eased. It was only a little, but it was still a relief. "Thank you."

Mira smiled. "You are too kind, Indra."

She had just nodded to the road in front of us when a Sovereign woman paused at our side. She was short, like me, and the robe she wore seemed to swallow her whole. Through the shadows the hood cast over her face, the woman's eyes seemed to crackle with fire when she looked Mira and me over.

"Move on," the woman snapped.

The Fortis guard who accompanied her everywhere she went stood at her back, large and imposing even among the swell of the crowd, but even more imposing was the electroprod clutched in the woman's hand. She pushed a button and the end of it buzzed to life as it glowed blue, growing brighter with each passing second, and at the sound even the Fortis man took a step away from her. The electroprod only needed to be on for a moment for it to work, but the longer it was on, the more intense the shock would be if the woman chose to use it. I had never experienced the pain of the shock personally, but I had seen men who were built as solidly as the walls surrounding this city fall to the ground from only a touch of the electroprod. That was all the motivation I needed.

I nodded once, careful to avoid the Sovereign woman's gaze. "Yes. Sorry."

The woman said nothing else, and so I turned away from her, grabbing Mira's arm as I did. Together we hurried through the crowd, pushing forward with our sights set on the gate. We were both trembling, but the closer we got to the gate, the more the tension began to ease.

When I was sure we had left the Sovereign woman behind, I released Mira's arm and slowed. My friend did as well, and once again we were walking side by side.

"Do you know who you are going to choose?" Mira

asked after only a moment of silence.

I let out a deep breath, blowing the remaining tension from my body before saying, "I was thinking of Ronan."

Mira's mouth morphed into a smile, brightening her already sparkling eyes. "He would be a good choice."

The boy was small for his age, but strong-willed and determined. He was only ten, but he had been single-handedly taking care of his mother and two young sisters since their father died last year. This job would give him a break and allow him to provide more for his family without working nearly as hard. It would mean that they would have more than most of the people in our village.

"I wish I could do more," I whispered.

"We all do," she said, speaking as quietly as I had, and then we both lapsed into silence.

Mira and I remained quiet the rest of the way through Sovereign City. The walk from Saffron's house to the wall was the only time during the day that we were able to really relax. The workday was done and the city streets were clean and safe. Peaceful even.

Of course, it had felt different at first. Back when I had first come to Sovereign City, the closeness of everything and the way the buildings and walls had towered over my head made me feel trapped. Everything had felt cold to me back then, fake. Not a drop of nature was visible inside the walls. The streets and houses were made of the same gray stone as the wall, and the buildings were so close together and high that it had felt as if they were bearing down on me, threatening to crush me or trap me here. Everything in the city was clean and maintained, but it was all gray, all stone.

As cold and lifeless as Saffron's eyes. It was overwhelming to a person who had grown up in the wilds.

Once I had gotten used to it all, I found an appreciation for the buildings in this city. They were all the same gray stone, but each was ornate in its own way, with arched doors and stained glass windows that added a touch of color to the otherwise drab city. Even after hundreds of years they were solid and impressive, a remnant from a time long gone and almost forgotten.

The clouds gathering in the distance had darkened the sky enough that the streetlights flicked on as Mira and I walked, casting circles of light on the road. I looked up, still awed even after all these years by the electric lights. It was hard to imagine a life where light was provided by just a flick of a switch, where water could be warmed without starting a fire, or a hot bath drawn for no reason other than the simple pleasure of allowing water to relax you. These were luxuries unknown to my people. Unknown to anyone but the Sovereign.

Mira and I were not the only ones heading home, and when we reached the gate we discovered that the line to get out of the city was twice as long as usual. She stood on her toes, peering over the heads of those in front of us so she could get an idea of what was taking so long. Usually it had something to do with the Fortis manning the gate. Most would never risk losing their positions by causing trouble inside the city, not when there were plenty of opportunities to bother Outliers outside the walls, but occasionally the men and women at the gate decided to have a little fun. They knew they could get away with it since very few of the

Sovereign would ever come this close to the gate.

"See anything?" I asked Mira, who was nearly a head taller than me.

"Not really." She exhaled and her breath came out in a puff of steam. "I wish they would hurry."

The clouds had thickened even more in the distance, and the air had chilled, but the sun beating down on us was still warm. A snowflake landed on the hair of the girl in front of us, melting within seconds thanks to the sun. Both Mira and I lifted our faces to the sky as more of the delicate flecks dropped from the clouds, and the bite in the air told me that it was already falling much heavier in our village.

Mira's gaze moved to my hands. "How are they?"

"Fine." I looked down, cringing at the welts on my skin.

My mother and Anja would be beside themselves when I got home, but I was telling the truth. The sting had lessened now that I was no longer folding laundry and scrubbing bathroom floors, and the chilly air had helped even more. My hands would still be tender tomorrow, but nothing like today. I was strong enough to work through the pain.

"By the time we get home there should be some snow," Mira said. "That will help. And Adina will have something to take even more of the sting out."

The line moved forward and I caught a glimpse of the Fortis guards working the gate. They opened it to let a few of their own men out, the one who had almost caught me when I stumbled included. He glanced back as he passed through and our eyes met. But I had been trained since childhood to look away, so it was only for the briefest of moments before my gaze was once again focused on the ground. It was not until I had looked down that I realized it did not matter, but by the time I looked back up he had disappeared through the gate and the doors were once again being pulled shut.

That left only five people separating Mira and me from freedom, three Fortis men and two Outlier women. They were from a different tribe, not that anyone inside the walls knew or cared, and both were older than Mira and me. Closer to my mother's age. The Fortis barely paid attention to the women before waving for them to move on, but when the guards turned their gazes on us, the predatory light in their eyes had my defenses up.

"Come on," the man closest to us barked.

Like all Fortis, he was large. Broad shouldered with a neck as wide as his head. His hair was as dark as the black uniform jacket he wore and had been slicked back and pulled into a tail at the base of his head. His brown, almost black, eyes zeroed in on Mira and me as we stepped forward, sweeping over us so fast that I was unsure if he was really seeing us.

At least not until he said, "New protocol. Arms up."

"Arms up?" Mira asked, sounding as startled as I felt.

We had just seen the two older Outlier women make it out of the city with no problem, and even though new laws were put in place all the time, we were usually informed of them. We had heard nothing about this, though.

"You heard him," the second Fortis man barked. He was wider than the first man, with the same dark clothes that made him seem twice as large, only his hair was a disheveled mop of blond that hung loose to the middle of his back.

Mira swallowed but complied, lifting her arms and

allowing the first man to pat her down.

I did the same with the second man, and as his hands moved down my body, a gust of wind swept down the street, sending a shiver shooting through me. At least I thought it was the wind. It was impossible to say for sure if it was from the cold or the situation, which was both preposterous and beyond my control. I knew as well as these men did that there were no new regulations. They were just bored and wanted to put us in our place.

The blond man started at my arms and worked his way down, patting my body so slowly and thoroughly that I felt as violated as I had that day in the pantry with Lysander. I sank my teeth into my lower lip, biting back words that were begging to get out because I knew they would get me nowhere. Causing a scene would not make the Sovereign sympathize with me. All they wanted was for their perfect little world to keep spinning undisturbed. Even worse, if I fought back this man would most likely take me into the headquarters, which was little more than a dark, windowless building. I had heard rumors of the horrors that happened within those walls whispered among the Outliers in Saffron's house, and I refused to give this man an excuse to get me in there.

Thankfully, the ordeal was over as fast as it had begun, and then Mira and I were on our way out. She was shaking, and I wrapped my arms around her as we passed out of Sovereign City and into the Fortis village, hoping the hug would calm not just her, but me as well.

FOUR

L EAVING THE CITY AFTER A CONFRONTATION
with the Fortis should have been a relief, but the sights
and sounds that hit the second we stepped through
the gate defied the relief escape brought.

The Fortis lived a rough and rowdy life, and their village
was so close to the wall that it was a miracle the chaos did
not make it into the city. The wall did its job, though. The
stone structure was twenty feet high and four feet thick, and
had been built to make certain that no one got in uninvited,
and nothing — not man or sound — could penetrate it.

Like the Outliers, the Fortis worked hard to ensure that
Sovereign City was spotless, but their efforts stopped at the
gate, almost as if the wall was somehow able to trap
motivation inside the city as thoroughly as it did privilege.
The stench of rotting food and too many people living
together was difficult, if not impossible, to ignore when

passing through the Fortis village. Add to that the stink of waste, both from animals and people, and it created a perfume of human misery that never failed to make my eyes water.

Out here the streets were not paved, the houses were not ornate or maintained, and most of the people made no effort to take care of themselves despite a ready supply of water. There was a standard of living inside the walls, so those who held positions inside the city did better, but everyone else looked as if they had given up trying decades ago. Not only were they filthy, but they also reeked of body odor and had teeth that were rotten to nubs. Those who had not shaved their heads completely—either for convenience sake or to escape an infestation of some kind of vermin—had knotted hair that often went down to the middle of their backs, and the beards of the Fortis men were pretty much the same.

As far as I knew, the only thing anyone in this village ever put any effort into was training. It started in youth regardless of gender, and continued on until a person was too old or too sick to keep going. The Fortis had been charged with guarding the city for centuries, and in exchange the Sovereign rewarded them with food and other supplies. As a result, these people were mountains, their already large bodies broad and bulging with muscles. As far as I knew, the Outliers had never attempted to defy the Sovereign, but if we had, we would be no match for the men and women who lived in this village. We were too weak, too malnourished, and looked like children compared to the men and women who lived in this village.

The Outliers that worked inside the city were forced to

walk through the Fortis Village to get to and from the gate, a task that was usually met with hostility and could turn dangerous if not careful. Outliers were cleaner and worked harder, and our villages were not cesspools of human garbage, but we were lower than the Fortis because we were less useful. These people kept watch over the wall and guarded the Sovereign, they hunted to provide those in the city with meat, and it made them necessary. We were too, assuming the people inside the walls wanted someone to cook and clean up after them, but there were four times as many Outliers as there were Fortis, and jobs inside were rare and nearly impossible to come by. Which meant that we were forced to scrape by if we wanted to survive.

Like every other day, Mira and I moved quickly through the Fortis Village, keeping our eyes straight ahead and ignoring the insults and suggestive comments tossed our way. The air was much chillier now, but the few flakes that managed to fall from the sky melted before they could collect on the ground. The Fortis were out in droves by the time we reached the halfway point, a section of the village that was marked by an open area and was often crowded with people. Today was no exception. If anything, the crowd appeared to be much larger than usual.

I pulled Mira closer to me when we were forced to squeeze our way through the men and women gathered in the center of the village. The stench of unwashed bodies was strong, but not strong enough to cover the scent of alcohol that wafted through the air as people laughed and flung abuse at us.

"Keep moving," I whispered to Mira.

She nodded and walked with me as I tried to move faster, elbowing my way through the crowd. Avoiding eye contact was the only defense I had against drawing more attention our way, but there were so many people that it felt like an impossible feat. I had to look up to see where I was going because the ground had been blocked from my view, and when I did I spotted the guard from Saffron's house again. For just a moment, his face was there amongst the crowd, and then he was gone, disappearing into a sea of Fortis men and women.

I searched for him for a beat before I realized there was no reason for me to look for him, and then I kept moving, pulling Mira with me until we had surfaced from the crowd. Then we began to run, the sound of laughter chasing us until we had made it to the edge of the Fortis Village where the wastelands and Lygan Cliffs stretched out before us.

Mira and I were out of breath when we stopped. The echoes of the Fortis still reached us from the village, but we knew none of them would bother to come after us. Still, I found myself looking back as Mira knelt down and tipped over the rock in front of her. Under it, in a shallow hole that had been dug centuries ago, were our weapons. We were prohibited from carrying them into the city, but traveling unarmed through the borderland that separated the wastelands from the Lygan Cliffs was dangerous, so we stashed the weapons here every morning on our way to work, collecting them again before making our long trek home. Mira and I had only had to use the knives a handful of times over the years, but they were instances that would have left us dead if we had been caught unarmed.

She passed me a knife, the hilt of which was rough against my sensitive palm, and then flipped the rock back over, covering the weapons the other people from our village had left. Then she stood, and together we did a quick survey of the area.

To our left the wastelands stretched on as far as the eye could see, the dry, cracked dirt only broken up by the occasional mound of boulders or skeleton tree. Their trunks were bleached white from the sun, and their limbs stretched up toward the sky as if begging God to save them from their desolate existence. The wastelands were less dangerous during the day since most of the creatures that inhabited them hunted at night in hopes of avoiding the oppressive heat from the sun, but with the chill in the air from the impending snow, anything was possible and it was better to be prepared than caught by surprise.

The Lygan Cliffs to our right held the greater threat, though. The cliffs were named for the creatures that lived there: scaly animals that were no bigger than a toddler but had teeth and claws sharp enough to slice a person open in seconds. Lygan were beautiful, their scales shades of purple and red that reflected the sun as they moved, but they were quick and deadly as well. They hunted both day and night, and had been known to work in packs. We had encountered them only a few times during my three years of working in Sovereign City, one of which had left Mira with a long scar on her left arm and in debt to Saffron for the replacement of her uniform, but we were always on the lookout. Thankfully, the arrival of a lygan was usually announced by the clicking of its claws against the very rocks it lived on.

The stone that made up the cliffs was jagged and sharp, and as black as night. They towered over us and dropped off in a steep cliff on the other side that ended in a valley. It was the same valley that Sovereign River ran through, starting in the wilds and ending in a large lake just outside the city. The river thrived with fish and other water creatures, which was why we were safer walking home this way, between the cliffs and the wastelands. When the lygan ventured from the rocks, it was usually to the river to hunt.

"It seems clear," I told Mira, still looking around.

The wastelands were as brown as usual, the snow melting too quickly once it landed on the hot ground to collect there, but the Lygan Cliffs were already peaked in the stuff. The black stone contrasted with the white that had collected there, telling me that by the time we had made the long journey home, the wilds would be covered in snow.

"We should get moving," Mira said.

She lifted her gaze to the sky, scanning the dark clouds that had collected over the wilds. The trees that indicated Outlier land were visible from here, their branches as bare now during winter as the skeleton trees' branches were. In the spring the greenery of the wilds was blinding compared to the desolate nothingness of the wastelands, and when they were covered in snow the sight was just as brilliant, but at the moment they looked very similar to the long dead trees to our left.

We remained alert as we started for home, my right hand aching every step of the way thanks to the way the knife rubbed against my palm, but I held onto it. At my right Mira blocked me from the Lygan Cliffs, which I knew was intentional. I appreciated her efforts more than I could ever tell her, knowing that if one of the creatures that inhabited those rocks decided to come down now I would have a difficult time defending myself thanks to the welts on my hands.

Before long the trail curled west, leading us further from the cliffs and allowing us to breathe a little easier. Then we were passing out of the wastelands and moving into Outlier territory and what was known as the wilds. The trees may have shed their leaves for the winter, but the grass was still green under the dusting of snow now covering the ground, and there was other foliage everywhere, like pines and bushes that clung to their leaves despite the cold.

The forest thickened and we once again found ourselves in familiar territory, but we still had a ways to walk before we reached home. Our tribe, the Winta, lived deep in the wilds.

There were four Outlier tribes, each of us numbering in the hundreds, but we were staggered throughout the wilds. Mira and I had already passed the Mountari territory at the edge of the Lygan Cliffs, and the Huni, who lived where the wastelands met the wilds. As Winta, our tribe interacted with the members of these tribes only in the city where it was unavoidable, but we had a little more contact with the fourth tribe, the Trelite, who lived the furthest from Sovereign City and shared more of our customs. Even that, however, was limited. Inside the wall we may have all been labeled Outliers, but in the wilds we had our own lives and customs, and the four tribes rarely, if ever, mixed.

The trees broke up as we stepped into the clearing that was our village. Just as I had thought, there was a fine dusting of snow on the ground. I had spent the last leg of our walk with my hands out in front of me, allowing the flakes to fall on my palms while Mira scooped up handfuls of snow that had gathered at the bottom of trees to place on the welts. As a result, some of the sting was gone by the time we crossed the threshold of our village, and the swelling had gone down significantly. I knew Adina, the village healer, would have something to help with the sting even more than the snow had, and I planned to make a visit to her once I let my mother and Anja know I was home.

Our huts stood tall and dark against the white blanket, dozens upon dozens of them. Smoke rose through the holes in the roofs of most, indicating that the families had settled in for the night. Here and there a person was visible: hauling wood in from the forest, patching a hole in their roof that had gone unnoticed before the snow began to fall, or dragging a kill in from the woods after a day of hunting. I spied Bodhi in the distance doing just this, his blond hair wild and wavy as he crossed the village and headed to his hut. A forest cat was draped over his shoulders, its fur as white as the snow. I found my gaze following his progress as Mira and I moved deeper into the village. It was always this way with Bodhi. He had been my closest friend during childhood, but had evolved into something else over the last few years. He was a man now who possessed muscles that boasted of his masculinity, and a smile that could wrap itself around my heart when it was directed my way.

"Will you talk to Ronan tonight?" Mira asked as we

slowed to a stop in front of my hut, tearing my thoughts from Bodhi.

Like all the others in our village, my home was primitive compared to the houses in Sovereign City, and even those in the Fortis village. We made our huts out of branches and sticks, packing the gaps with mud in an effort to keep the weather out. The roof was much the same, made of layers upon layers of sticks, followed by mud and large leaves, with a small hole in the center to vent the smoke from our fires. The hut I shared with my mother and sister was smaller than the dining room in Saffron's house, but provided more than enough space for the three of us to live comfortably. Even before my father's death there had been more than enough room.

"Yes," I said, my gaze searching the village for Bodhi again. He had disappeared, though I had no doubt that I would see him later. "Saffron wants to meet Ronan as soon as possible, and as long as his mother can spare him tomorrow, he will come with us in the morning."

"He will be pleased." Mira's smile remained firm, but the sadness in her eyes told me how much she wished her own brother could have the position.

"He will." I turned toward my hut when guilt over not being able to do more squeezed my insides. It was unfair, and out of my control just like most things in life were, but it still made me ache for the pain of my people. "I will see you tomorrow, Mira."

Both my mother and Anja were inside when I stepped through the door. Our mother lay on the bed with a thick fur curled around her body and her arms stuck out so she could hold a bowl of stew. The bed was made of animal hides and stuffed with leaves and other foliage from the forest. It was thin and narrow. Nothing like the huge, soft things the Sovereign slept on, and I felt a pang in my chest yet again when I thought about how much more comfortable she would have been in one of those beds. How much more rest she would have been able to get.

When my mother saw me, she paused in her eating and smiled. "Indra."

As always, all it took was the gentle tone of her voice to make me feel at home. To help me feel safe.

My sister looked up from where she sat on the floor, the pot of stew in front of her and a bowl in her own hand, and smiled as well. When Anja set her bowl down and moved to prepare one for me, I waved for her to stop. She froze, her eyes on my hands.

"I am okay," I told her.

The stew now forgotten, Anja stood and crossed the small distance to me. "Let me see."

My sister was younger than me by six years, but taller and lankier, all wiry muscles while I was slim enough to be able to pass for a child. Anja took after our mother, who was her real mother but mine only because she chose me. They both had the same deep brown skin, dark eyes, and black hair, which they kept cut close to their scalps. Their skin was as dark as mine was light, and with my hands held in my sister's, my flesh looked as pale as the snow that was at this very moment covering the ground outside our hut.

The only similarities my sister and I shared were the passage markings above our eyebrows, four dots that signified the family we belonged to, and the half circle on our cheeks that had been given to us upon our father's death. Unlike her, I had a line above mine that indicated the loss of my birth parents as well. I had come into this family when I was just a baby, but from where or whom I did not know or care. Dichen was the only mother I had ever known, and there were too many daily concerns to worry myself about people I would never meet.

My mother frowned up at me from her place on the bed. "Saffron had a bad day?"

"I think I am the one who had a bad day," I told her, but I knew what she meant.

As much as I had refused to admit it to Mira earlier, I knew that I was Saffron's favorite. She may have enjoyed inflicting pain, but she also prided herself in how compliant I was. It was why I was loaned out to other houses more often than anyone else, why Saffron had asked me to find a Hand for Lysander. She felt that I could be molded better than most, which I supposed was true. I did as I was told and made sure it was done well. In Sovereign City, there was no room for error. Not when I had family depending on me.

"Does it hurt much?" Anja asked.

I shook my head as I pried my hands from hers and started undoing the buttons on my dress. The motion stung, but I worked to keep my face expressionless. Just like in the city, I did what I could to control my emotions. It would do no one any good for me to show my pain.

"I am fine, and I will be even better after I see Adina. I only stopped in to change and let you know that I made it home okay."

Anja remained rooted to the floor even after I had turned away and pulled my dress over my head. I grabbed my own clothes, made from animal hides that were thick and would do a better job of protecting me from the cold. The fur that trimmed my shirt was soft against my skin, and being in it made me feel better. Not just warmer, but more comfortable because I was home with my family and wearing my own clothes.

My sister was still watching me when I turned, so I grabbed her and pulled her in for a hug. "Eat, Anja." I lifted myself onto the tips of my toes and kissed the top of her head the way I had when we were both young and she was still shorter than me, and the fibers of her hair tickled my lips. "I am fine."

Anja did as I said and returned to the floor while our mother watched me from the bed. It was then that I noticed how ashen her complexion was compared to my sister's, and how sunken her eyes had begun to look. The black passage markings she wore stood out against her dark skin more than ever before, the swirls over her eyebrows for the family she had been born into, the dots and lines in the center of her forehead that she had received on her wedding day, and the numerous markings on her cheeks that showed how much loss she had suffered during her lifetime. Too much for one person.

I took a seat at her side and felt her forehead, and was rewarded by the feel of cool skin against mine. She leaned her head against my damaged palm, and not even the smallest sting accompanied the gentle gesture.

"Are you feeling okay?" I asked.

"I should be asking you that," she said. "I am the mother."

"But I have already told you that I am okay."

She nodded, relenting. "I am fine, child. Go see Adina. Get something for your pain."

"I will."

I stood, but stayed where I was. I had things to do, but I found myself wishing that I could curl up on the bed beside my mother the way I had when I was young. It was impossible though, not right now anyway.

"I also need to stop by Ronan's hut," I said. "Saffron is looking for a Hand for Lysander, and she has asked me to choose someone."

My mother's face broke out into a smile, revealing teeth that were startlingly white beside her dark skin. "His family will be pleased."

"And there are others who will be furious with me for not choosing them."

Voicing my concerns did nothing to ease my worry the way I had hoped it would. I knew nothing could, but I also realized that I was not responsible for the things that happened. The opposite, really. I had no control over them. There was nothing I could do to ease the burden the Outliers carried, or pull them out of poverty and starvation, and I could not offer them more than they already had. I wanted to, so much, but it was not within my power. There were too many obstacles in my way, both as an Outlier and a Winta woman.

My mother reached up to grab my hand, giving just the tip of my fingers a gentle squeeze. "You cannot make everyone happy no matter how hard you try."

"I know," I said with a sigh.

"But you always try anyway," she replied with a knowing smile on her face.

"I always try anyway," I agreed, but unlike my mother, I found smiling impossible.

FIVE

ADINA GAVE ME A SALVE FOR MY WOUNDS, promising that I would be as good as new within a couple days. It was an impossible thing to promise, being as good as new, when we never had enough to go around. Life in the city was lavish, gluttonous and excessive. Their scraps were tossed to the Fortis, both to keep the men and women who guarded them strong, but also to maintain their loyalty. In contrast, we had to work hard for everything we were given. And there was very little work available. The Sovereign controlled the Fortis, using them to control everything else without even having to lift a finger.

The Outliers without jobs in the city hunted or gathered, but game could be sparse in the wilds. Most of the animals kept close to the river, which was Fortis territory. Inside the city the Sovereign grew food in climate-controlled buildings, giving them light and artificial rain whenever it was needed, but in the wastelands that surrounded the walls, nothing grew. The wilds were slightly better, but even here the earth grew crops very poorly, as if whatever had stripped the wastelands of their fruitfulness had poisoned our soil as well. Things had improved over the years, like the earth was slowly evicting the toxins from its depths, but we still had times when everything we planted shriveled before it could be harvested. Or worse, bore fruit that made us sick when we ate it.

I was one of the lucky few who had a position inside Sovereign City, a fact I tried to remind myself of as I rubbed the salve onto my aching palms. Most of the time it was easy, but there were moments, like this one, when it was a tough blessing to swallow. When it was difficult to remember that luck had brought me this pain, and that because of it my family was better off than others.

Ronan's hut was on the far side of the village, and after getting the salve I headed there instead of home. Flakes still fell from the sky and the air had cooled even more with the setting of the sun, but the various fires burning throughout the village helped keep some of the chill away and prevented too much of the snow from collecting between the huts. Still, I longed to be back inside with my family so I could eat some hot stew and curl up on the bed to keep warm. So I could lick the wounds the day had inflicted upon me and allow myself a few quiet hours to heal.

Halfway through the village I caught sight of Emori. She was headed my way, a basket of pine needles under one arm and a belly so swollen that it strained against her clothes. The sight of her always made my insides flip, and today was no exception. She did not blame me, I knew that for sure, but it was much more difficult to forgive myself for what had happened. I had been in the kitchen when Lysander stepped into the pantry behind her, I had heard the door click shut and the sound of her cries, and I had done nothing to stop him.

Tears pricked at my eyes, and despite my earlier decision to talk to her about Isa, I found myself ducking between a couple of huts to avoid her. I swiped the back of my hand across my face as I went, hating that I felt so weak and out of control when I thought of that day, but knowing it would never change. Emori had needed my help, but I had done nothing. There had been nothing I could do, something I knew all too well, but the injustice of the situation did nothing to alleviate my self-loathing, just as I was sure the women who had been in the kitchen three years ago when Lysander cornered me felt the same way. We were not responsible, but in the absence of someone else to put the blame on, we had taken it upon ourselves.

I felt even more like a coward as I wove my way between huts in an effort to avoid Emori, but I did it anyway. The day had been emotional enough without throwing another log on the fire burning inside me, and at the moment all I wanted to do was talk to Ronan so I could get home to my family and wrap myself in their comforting embrace.

As he often did, Bodhi had something else in mind completely, and I had only made it a little further when he suddenly appeared in front of me, stepping out from between a few huts and blocking my way.

I stopped only inches from him, feeling his nearness more than usual thanks to my already emotional state. Outliers in general were taller than the Sovereign, although thin and wiry, but Bodhi was not a tall man. Still, next to my small frame he felt large. Especially in moments like this when I found myself feeling so helpless and weak. Usually, I found his presence calming, even more so than my mother and sister at times, or Mira. Bodhi and I had been friends for as long as I could remember, often spending the entire day together when were small. Now though, with my emotions swirling and my palms still stinging from my punishment, I found myself wishing to avoid him. I knew why. He could see through me better than anyone else and he knew me so well that I could hide nothing from him, and right now that was all I wanted to do. Hide.

His blue eyes swept over me, and without having to utter a word, he seemed to know what I had been through. He took my hands in his and turned them over so my palms were facing up. In the flickering light of the nearby fire, the welts on my skin appeared red and angry. But his skin was warm under mine. Comforting and familiar.

He said nothing, but instead leaned down and pressed his lips against each one of my palms. I was crying by that point, and when Bodhi wrapped his arms around me and pulled me against him, the sobs came faster and harder. The sting of the welts was only half of it. Seeing Emori had opened up a part of me that I liked to keep buried, but I was not a fool. Both the tears and my desire to avoid her were as much about my own time in the pantry with Lysander as they were about hers. It was easier to project that moment onto someone else though, to imagine that I had always been outside the door, powerless but less of a victim than the person inside. It could not change the truth, could not change the fact that I had at one time also been at Lysander's mercy, but it did make it easier for me to get through the day. Easier to continue to do the work expected of me inside the city and pretend that the things I witnessed there left no mark on me. It made it easier for me to be the clay people like Saffron wished to mold.

When my tears had slowed, Bodhi stepped back. He kept his hands on my shoulders and looked me over. A few tendrils of hair fell across my forehead, damp from the swiftly falling snow, and I reached up to shove them out of my face. He beat me to it though, and the brush of his fingers against my forehead was gentle and soothing, as was the expression in his blue eyes. It made my heart pound faster. Made my mind wander.

I had grown up running from Bodhi as we played, and then for other reasons as we got older. At this point I felt as if I had been running from him for years, and yet he never tired of the chase. Had never given up hoping that he might one day catch me and make me his. I knew this just as surely as everyone else in the village did, and as much as I could not deny the fact that I yearned for him, I was not ready to stop running. Not yet, anyway.

"I hate what you go through in there." The tiny ball in his throat bobbed when he swallowed, and his grip on my shoulders tightened.

"It is no different than what anyone else has to endure," I said. "We are only Outliers. We are nothing."

"You are everything to me," he whispered. "I would prove that to you if you would let me."

His eyes, as blue as the sky, held mine as icy air whipped between the huts and rustled his wavy hair. The passage markings above his eyebrows were the only ones he had, and I found myself thinking that his misguided belief that he could fix all of my problems with only his love had something to do with that. He had no marks for the people he had lost because he had never lost anyone. His parents were alive, as were his two brothers. He hunted every day because he wanted to help his family and the whole village, not because he had to. Not because he was the head of a family who depended on him. Still, there was something very comforting about a person who was determined to make everything perfect, no matter how unrealistic that goal was. Truth be told, *everything* about Bodhi was warm and comforting. So why did I insist on running from him?

"If I could, I would go into the city and kill them all," he whispered.

"They would catch you and then you would die."

Terror twisted in my gut at the thought of Bodhi dying, and I suddenly knew why the idea of letting him love me frightened me so much. It would mean letting him in. If we got married he would swear to protect me, just as all the Winta men did when they took a wife. Only Bodhi would take the promise to heart. He would think it was his duty to right any wrong done to me, no matter the cost. Even if it meant going into Sovereign City and getting himself killed.

"There is nothing you can do," I said, and wiggled out of his grasp. "Trust me."

I started to walk again, and as always he followed.

"Will you never tire of chasing me?" I asked after a few beats of silence.

"I told you I never would."

I glanced his way out of the corner of my eye. "Why? Why me?"

"Do you not know?" Bodhi turned so he was facing me, walking sideways, and the crooked smile he shot me penetrated the wall around my heart. "Because you are better than every other woman in this village. Smarter and stronger, and braver too. I knew it when we were five years old and you went into the woods with me. I have always known it."

Heat flared at my cheeks and I looked away. "I am nothing special, Bodhi."

"You are everything to me, Indra."

I stopped walking, finding myself staring at him in shock. He did not blink, and he held my gaze, totally unashamed that he had said those words.

"One day you will decide to let me catch you, and when I do, I will never let you go," he finally said. "For now, I will give you your space."

He turned away but I stayed where I was, watching him, still unable to react to the things he had just said. For years Bodhi had been open about his intentions, about wanting to marry me so he could take care of me for the rest of my life, but he had never been as open as he was just now. Had never been so close to confessing his feelings to me.

I started walking again when Bodhi disappeared from view, making my way to Ronan's hut. Now that my insides were a tangled mess of emotions, I was more anxious than ever to get back to my family.

The boy answered the door when I knocked. His skin was as freckled as mine, and the dark shadows under his gray eyes had no place on a child so young. Knowing that I was about to take some of the burden from his shoulders helped push away some of my guilt at not offering the job to one of the dozens of other boys I knew, and the sound of one of his younger sisters crying pushed the rest of my remorse away. By the time I let Ronan and his mother know why I had come, I was confident in my decision, and I was able to accept their enthusiastic thanks with almost no guilt.

"You will have to leave the village very early tomorrow," I told him. "But you can travel with Mira and me until you learn what your hours will be."

"Will we be going through the wastelands?" he asked, and I was unsure if the energy in his voice was from fear or excitement.

"We travel the borderland between the wastelands and the Lygan Cliffs. It is safer, but there can still be trouble. You will have to be on alert." I took a deep breath then. This was the hardest part, preparing the boy for what he was about to face without scaring him. "Just as you will need to be inside the city. You must listen very carefully to what I tell you, Ronan. Are you listening?"

The boy's eyes had gotten big, but he nodded.

"While in the city you must obey any order the Sovereign or Fortis give you," I said firmly. "No matter what. Do you understand?"

He nodded again, this time so hard that his shaggy

brown hair flopped across his forehead, covering the passage markings above his right eye. "Yes."

"You are just an Outlier in there," I continued. "Which means you are nothing. You must not speak unless spoken to. You do your work and never question anyone or talk back. You never take extra food, even if it is to be thrown in the waste. You must never touch any of the Sovereign's belongings unless they tell you to, and even then there will be times when you are punished. No one escapes the wrath of the Sovereign forever. But if you do your best and listen to what I have told you, the reprimand will be minor." I held my hands out so he could see the welts lining my palms. "Larger crimes bring severe punishment. Floggings. Death. Remember that the Winta pride ourselves on being moral and trustworthy. Do not bring shame to our tribe or it will follow you into the afterlife."

Ronan was still listening, his eyes as big as they had been when I first began, but I felt as if I needed to make sure he understood that it was not *all* bad. That even though he would be whipped a time or two, this job would mean a better life for his family.

"The job is harsh, but you will be paid well. You are given food rations every day to keep you strong, and at the end of every week you will be given more to bring back to your family. Grain, fruit, and vegetables that the Sovereign grow in special buildings within the walls. Things that we cannot get in the wilds because the soil does not allow it. This will not always be an easy job, but it will be worth it if you think you can follow the rules. Can you?"

"I can do it, Indra. Thank you." Ronan's eyes were still wide when he nodded, but they were also full of sincerity, and I felt certain that he was taking my words to heart. That he understood what was at stake.

"You are welcome, Ronan." I stood to leave. "Be sure you are ready to go at sunrise. The trip is long and we cannot be late."

SIX

ONAN WAS TRUE TO HIS WORD, AND THE NEXT morning I found him waiting for me at the edge of the village.

He was chipper on our way to the city, seemingly undeterred by the numerous warnings Mira and I threw his way, both about the dangers we could encounter on our walk and what he would face inside Saffron's house. He remained animated until the wall finally came into view, but even then I was uncertain if it was from fear, or because the sight of the massive stone structure overwhelmed him.

I understood his enthusiasm even though I no longer shared it. As a child, the idea of going into Sovereign City, even as a servant, had been enthralling. I had never seen the walls, it was much too dangerous to travel the borderland for no reason, but I had heard them described dozens of times throughout my life. My mother had started training me for the job at a young age to ensure that I would be ready, something I did not think much of until years later when she fell sick. It was as if she had known even that far back that she would be called into the afterlife much too early.

It had taken less than an hour inside the walls for me to realize that I was not as blessed as I had thought, though. Yes, we were lucky to have the position, but with the job came great sacrifice. More than I ever could have imagined. I had no doubt that Ronan would be faced with the same epiphany before long.

We showed him where to stash his weapons when we reached the end of the borderland, knowing that he would most likely be on a different shift and therefore not travel with us after today. I warned him yet again to never take a weapon into the city, praying that he heeded not just this, but all the warnings I had showered him with during the long walk, and then we set off again.

The Fortis village made Ronan uneasy like nothing else yet had, and as I compared him to the hulking men we passed, I understood why. He was small enough that I was certain he could be crushed under the boots of some of these men if they decided he was in need of being stomped on, and once again I found myself whispering instructions to him. Warning him to keep his head down, to never look one of the Fortis in the eye if he could avoid it. To do everything he was told without question.

When we arrived at the House of Saffron, I escorted the boy to her office where the mistress inspected him as if he were a strip of meat she was considering serving to important guests. Ronan stood still during the whole procedure, doing as I had instructed him and saying nothing unless addressed directly, and for his restraint I was grateful. If he messed up on the first day not only would he lose the position, but I might also be punished for bringing him into the city. My hands had mostly healed thanks to Adina, but receiving a whipping on top of the welts from yesterday would no doubt tear the skin this time around.

"He's a very small child," Saffron said with a frown, and then looked at me. "Is he hard working?"

The way she talked about the boy as if he wasn't even present made me grind my teeth, but as usual I swallowed my annoyance down.

"He is very hard working," I told her. "His father died last year and Ronan has been providing for his mother and two younger sisters by foraging in the forest all day. He gets up before the sun and is awake long after it has set."

"At ten?" Saffron nodded in approval. "That is very impressive." She waved to him as she turned away. "Very well. You may escort him to the kitchen so the housemaid can get him a uniform."

I curtsied even though Saffron was no longer looking at us, careful to keep my head down when I said. "Thank you, mistress."

"Thank you, mistress," Ronan repeated obediently.

We left the office, the boy trailing behind me, and I caught sight of the guard who had asked me if I was okay only the day before. He was standing by the front door, staring at me with dark eyes that stayed focused on me the whole way across the room. Despite the fact that I usually avoided looking at the guards, his expression was so intense and his gaze so engrossed that I found myself glancing back every few seconds, shocked each time I did because he was still looking at me.

It happened again later in the day, during lunch service this time. I was serving the potatoes when I happened to look toward the Fortis lined up at the back of the room and found the man watching me with an identical expression in his eyes, his gaze just as unyielding as it had been earlier.

The behavior continued throughout the meal, putting me so much on edge that I had a difficult time keeping my hands from shaking as I cleared the dirty plates. Why did he insist on staring at me? Was this a new occurrence or something I simply had not noticed before now? I had never paid much attention to the men and women charged with guarding the family, but I knew for certain that this man had been working in the house as long as I had. Perhaps even longer. Like the Outliers, the Fortis were born into their positions, and he had probably replaced his father in the house. Unless there were extenuating circumstances, the Fortis rarely came into the city before their eighteenth birthday, and usually around twenty years of age. This man had to be several years older than me. Twenty-seven, perhaps older.

I would have asked him why he was staring at me if I had been braver, but I was not. Not only had I been trained to never talk to the Fortis, but I was also Winta. In my village, women were considered weak, and putting myself in a dangerous situation was out of the question. Especially when I had no father or husband to protect me.

Days passed and the situation remained the same. Even worse, once I noticed the Fortis man it seemed as if I was always on the lookout for him, wondering if he was standing in the shadows watching me pass or staring at me during meal service. When the guards came into the kitchen to have their daily lunch, I found myself torn between wanting to avoid looking in his direction and wanting to know if he was watching me yet again. It unnerved me, thinking about having this man watching me.

The Fortis despised Outliers almost as much as the Sovereign did, although in a much different way. The Sovereign saw us as beneath them. They looked at the markings on our skin, at the shaved heads and piercings of the Huni tribe, and the Lygan teeth the Mountari often decorated their skin with, and they saw savage customs. The Fortis, however, hated us for sport. They took joy in brutalizing any Outlier they came into contact with in the wilds, raping our women and beheading our men. It was a game to them, just as picking on our vulnerabilities inside the walls was. I was well aware of the brutal reputation the Fortis had, as well as the fact that it was justly deserved, and that reputation was exactly why the attention I was getting from the guard in Saffron's house concerned me so much.

Despite my worries, the man who persisted in watching me whenever we were in the same room together never gave even the smallest indication that he was dangerous. He never threatened me or tried to corner me, or even threw insults my way. Other than the day he had asked if I was okay, he never even spoke to me.

Weeks passed and I began to forget that he watched me so intently. Ronan had fallen into his job effortlessly, providing more for his family than he ever had before, and even Lysander seemed pleased with the boy's efforts. My time working in Saffron's House returned to normal, and I concentrated on working hard and keeping my head down, not wanting to draw attention to myself. It was the easiest way for an Outlier to get through the day inside Sovereign City. Work and do as you were told until it was time to leave, so that was what I did.

RONAN HAD BEEN WORKING IN THE HOUSE FOR nearly a month when a special dinner was held in honor of Lysander's impending marriage. His future wife was a waif, an anomaly among the Sovereign, and so thin she would have been at home in an Outlier village—assuming she would have survived even one night outside the walls, which I doubted. There were so few of the Sovereign, and with no new blood being introduced into the gene pool, small or sickly children became more common with each passing year. Although this woman was the worst case I had ever seen. How she would have two healthy babies I had no clue, but I knew it would be expected of her.

The Sovereign had run out of space to expand decades ago, and population control was closely regulated. Since both Lysander and his wife had come from a one child family, they would be expected to have two children of their own. The alternating generations kept the population from exploding while ensuring that the Sovereign would not die out anytime soon, and it was closely regulated and strictly enforced.

By contrast, Lysander was as plump as his father. His

small stature contrasted with the roundness of his frame, making it seem as if he would topple over with even the smallest shove, and yet when he had his sights set on something, or someone, he moved with a lethal quickness that could have rivaled a lygan. His round face, often sweaty, was already as waxy-looking as his parents' and had taken on a yellowish tint that was common among the men inside the city. Too much drinking I could only assume since that was how most of the men spent their days.

While Lysander ate his meal, Ronan stood dutifully at his master's side. Lysander probably did it on purpose. Anyone could tell just by looking at the boy that he often went without at home, and the sights and smells of the food were no doubt torturous for him. Lysander had inherited his mother's love for inflicting pain; only he had no qualms about showing it. Saffron at least had enough breeding to hide hers. For the most part.

I circled the table with a bottle of wine, pouring more into any glasses that needed refilling. Lysander waved his meaty hand to his half-empty glass when I walked by and I stopped at his side.

When his hand touched the back of my leg, I refused to react. Not when it moved up, not when it cupped the curve of my right buttock. Not when his fingers delved deeper, so deep they would have found a home inside me if not for the folds of my skirt. The small tremble of my hand was the only thing that gave me away, but even that was controlled. No, Lysander had never gotten me in the pantry a second time, but this was a common occurrence in Saffron's house.

"Indra," Saffron called from across the table.

Her son's hand fell away.

"Mistress?" I replied as I took a step back, putting distance between Lysander and myself.

"My son tells me that his new Hand is doing very well. As always, you have done an excellent job. Thank you."

"I am pleased that you are happy," I said, and then with my eyes cast down, I returned to my spot at Mira's side.

The statement was a power play for Saffron and had very little to do with Ronan or me. Stateswoman Paizlee just so happened to be the mother of Lysander's future wife—whose name I still had not caught—and Saffron was letting her political loyalties be known. Their children may be getting married, but supporting the Stateswoman's new bill was out of the question.

"You're lucky to have such good help." Paizlee dabbed at her mouth with a cloth napkin. She was a good decade younger than Saffron, and as round as a woman in her position was expected to be. "It hasn't been the case as of late, I'm afraid to say. The Outliers have become increasingly unreliable. They see their positions as a birthright and have therefore taken them for granted."

"Isn't that what they are?" Lysander asked through a mouthful of food. "A birthright?"

Both women looked at him before glancing at his soon-to-be-wife. She was staring at her hands, which were folded neatly in her lap. She was the most silent woman I had ever seen within the walls of the city. It was her complacent personality that had no doubt led Lysander to choose her as his bride. Bastian may have been satisfied to drink his days away and leave the important decisions to Saffron, but

Lysander was nothing like his father. He liked control.

"No." Paizlee dropped her napkin on the table. "These *people* have no rights, least of all birthrights. We allow them to keep the jobs in the family because it's easier for us. We know the mothers spend their evenings teaching their daughters, which means that by the time they come here they already know the rules. Isn't that how it was with your girl? What was her name? Idina?"

"Indra," Saffron corrected her. "And yes. She came to me three years ago well trained and ready to work. Her mother, Dichen, prepared her, so when she arrived it was only a matter of giving her a tour and handing her a uniform. The transition was flawless."

"Precisely," Paizlee said, pointing at the air to emphasize her point. "As it should be. Unfortunately, too many Outliers now look at it as a position they cannot lose, and they've become lazy and insolent as a result."

My back stiffened and Mira shot me a look. I had never met a single Outlier who was lazy. People who slacked off in the wilds died. We were nothing like the Sovereign, who would be unable to brew a cup of coffee if not for us.

Paizlee continued her rant about how ungrateful Outliers were while the rest of the room ate and drank in silence. Bastian was well on his way to consuming an entire bottle of wine by himself when he waved for me to refill his glass. Across from him, Paizlee's round husband, whose name I was even less sure of than I was his daughter's, was just as bad.

Dinners like this gave the men little to do other than drink. They were uninvolved in political matters, which was often the topic of conversation when Saffron got together with other women, and by this point in his life, Bastian had outlived his usefulness. He had given Saffron a child, which was the extent of his job in this house, and he was now free to live a life of ease. Which to him apparently meant drinking himself into an early grave.

I refilled his glass, and then the glass of Paizlee's husband, and was just about to return to my spot with the other servants when Lysander waved me over.

My head was down as I crossed the room to him, but I could feel his eyes on me every step of the way, and when I reached him I was unsurprised to find his glass still half full. He put one meaty finger up, signaling for me to wait, and then grabbed the glass, downing the rest of it quickly before setting it on the table. Only he set it on the opposite side of his plate, forcing me to step closer and lean over. This time when his hand moved up my leg, my hand trembled so much that I ended up dribbling wine on the white, lace tablecloth.

"Indra," Saffron snapped. Her eyes flicked to her son and she let out a sigh, the first sign she had ever given to indicate that she knew what he was up to. "Please be more careful."

"Yes, mistress. I apologize."

Curtsying gave Lysander the perfect opportunity to get his hand right where he wanted it. He wiggled his fingers and I had to bite back a yelp. His hand stayed there until I had taken a step back, and by then heat had crept up my neck to my face. I wanted to smash the bottle I was holding over his head. Wanted to hit him again and again until it broke his skull open and his blood painted the walls of this room.

Tears stung at my eyes and I squeezed the neck of the bottle tighter as I returned to my place. Just as I was passing the guard who had spent the last few weeks watching me, he shifted. My gaze flicked up and he captured it with his own, and in that moment I saw something I never thought I would see in the eyes of one of the guards. Sympathy. Even more surprising, was the rage I saw when he looked past me to the table.

SEVEN

T HE KITCHEN WAS QUIET AS WE CLEANED UP from the evening meal. Lysander had made his mark on every woman in the room tonight, me more than anyone. Even though I had known it was coming—wine duty when Lysander decided to grace the house with his presence usually came with consequences—it was still difficult to shake off.

We were still washing the dishes when the door behind us flew open and Saffron called out, "Dining room. Now."

I set the pot I was holding on the counter and at my side Mira did the same. When I turned, her gaze met mine.

"What do you think happened?" she asked.

Based on Saffron's tone, I guessed someone had done something wrong. Only I was uncertain what.

"She will let us know soon enough," I replied as I dried my hands.

Since I knew I had not betrayed the mistress's trust, I was unconcerned as I followed the other Outliers out of the kitchen. That changed the second I set foot in the dining room and found a teary-eyed Ronan standing at Saffron's side.

"No," I gasped as my steps faltered.

"Line up," Saffron snapped, her eyes surveying the room as we filed out. They seemed twice as cold as usual. Like icicles.

Behind her, sitting with his feet propped up on the table, Lysander wore a malicious smile. His electroprod sat across his lap, not on but ready in case anyone stepped out of line. Bastian, I knew, had gone to bed. He had been too drunk to even stand up by the time the meal had ended, and two guards had helped him up the stairs, a common occurrence in this house.

Mira grabbed my arm on her way by and practically pulled me across the room. The guards were lined up behind Saffron and Ronan, their eyes nearly as emotionless as hers. I searched the group until I found the man I was looking for, the one who had given me a sympathetic look earlier, only the expression he wore now was no different than the men and women around him. He was just as big and strong and looked just as heartless as every other guard in the room. Maybe I had imagined that he had ever been anything else.

Once we were all in place, Saffron stepped forward, leaving poor little Ronan to cry on his own. "Am I not a good mistress? Don't I give you everything you need?"

Unsure whether or not we were supposed to respond, the other maids and I remained silent.

Saffron continued without demanding an answer, confirming that we had made the right decision by holding our tongues. "I have told each and every one of you already, but let me reiterate it so you don't forget. As long as you don't betray my trust, you will have a position here, which means food and survival for your families. But—" She turned to face Ronan. "—if you betray me, you will face the consequences."

Ronan sniffed, but his head was still down. Without being able to get a good look at his face, it was impossible for me to gauge how bad the situation was. What had he done? Questioned Lysander? Talked back? Something like that would be small, a whipping across his hand, possibly to his backside, but if something more had happened, if he had done something bigger, the outcome could be much, much worse.

Saffron turned to face us and my blood ran cold when her icy gaze landed on me. This was bad, bigger than talking back. But how bad was it? It was hard to say, and impossible for me to imagine what he had done, especially after all the warnings Mira and I had showered him with. Whatever it was though, I felt certain that Ronan's life was about to be altered, maybe even taken from him.

"Ronan, who has been in my house for only a month," Saffron began after only a moment's pause, "was caught stealing. He was charged with gathering the leftover food after dinner, and in the process he slipped two rolls into his pockets." She looked us all over slowly, giving this news a moment to sink in before saying, "You all know the punishment for stealing, don't you?"

My heart thudded violently and I found myself stumbling forward, my head down but my eyes up just enough that I was able to see Saffron. "Mistress, please."

She frowned and behind her Lysander sat up, his stubby legs dropping to the floor with a thud.

"Are you defending his actions?" Saffron asked in a voice that was as icy as the snow.

Yes, I thought. *Yes, I am defending his actions. Not because stealing is okay, but because I have seen how he lives. I have seen his starving sisters and I know he only did this to save them.*

Out loud I said, "No, mistress. I am only asking that you show him mercy. He is just a child. He was wrong, but you can still show him mercy. Let him return home in shame. Losing the job will be enough of a punishment to teach him a lesson."

Saffron stepped closer to me and I was forced to lift my eyes from the floor. Her gaze was as cold as her tone, as cold as the stone this city was made out of. "Very few Outliers have the privilege of working in the city, and you know as well as I do that there are people within these walls who wish to change that. It goes beyond Stateswoman Paizlee's opinions. There are people who don't want your kind here at all, and they petition for your dismissal every day. If I show this boy mercy and it gets out, there will be outrage. It will feed the flames of change. I must do this for you and for your people. You have to know that."

I knew no such thing, but I did know what was expected of me and what needed to be done in order to keep my own job, so I bowed my head again, casting my eyes to the floor, and said, "Yes, mistress." And I hated myself for it.

She turned her back to me and I lifted my eyes just in time to see her nod to the guards. "Send word that there will be a gathering."

ALL ROADS INSIDE THE WALLS LED TO THE TOWN square, which sat in the very center of Sovereign City. If the purpose of this very open area had been something other than the humiliation of my people, it would have been the only place within the walls that did not feel suffocating. But all public activities were conducted in the square, including Outlier punishments. It was where the floggings took place, where the stocks were, and where Ronan would very soon pay the price for defying the Sovereign.

The square faced the city's government building, which was the tallest structure inside the walls. It was twice as high as all the other buildings and had a roof that pointed up toward the sky. I had never set foot inside it, but everyone knew this building was the center of Sovereign technology. They grew their food within those walls, in special rooms that had artificial light and rain, and they manufactured everything they needed inside as well. New clothes, shoes, medicine, and luxury items that seemed beyond frivolous to me. Everything that kept this city going was housed inside this building, and it was even rumored that the building was the source of their electricity, although no one knew that for certain. Outliers were allowed inside to harvest food and manufacture the items the Sovereign needed, but most of it was off limits to us, and therefore an utter mystery.

The crowd gathered in the square was already larger than I had expected it to be, with more people pouring in with each passing moment. Years had gone by since a punishment this severe had been dealt out, and despite my powerlessness, I felt the weight of it on my shoulders. I was the one who had chosen Ronan, had brought him into the city. This was my fault. I should have done a better job of warning him, should have made him understand how serious things could be for our people inside these walls. This punishment was on my hands as much, if not more, than it was on Saffron's, because I could have done more to make Ronan understand the danger he was in.

I stood at the back of the platform with the rest of the Outliers from Saffron's house. Mira and I had been forced to stay in the city beyond our work hours so we could witness the punishment. Not that we would have left Ronan. He would need help getting home after the ordeal was over, and as the one responsible for bringing him here, I would shoulder the burden.

The sun was already setting over the wastelands, and inside the walls the city had begun to darken. The streetlights were on, shining down on everyone who had gathered to watch. It was mostly the Sovereign who had come running at the news that a gathering had been called, but I spied a large number of Fortis in the crowd as well, towering over the robed figures crammed into the square. Even though the sun was now low in the sky, they still wore the robes as if the heavy fabric was necessary to protect them from the brutal sun. No Outliers would come here unless they were forced to, and thankfully, it seemed as if most had been allowed to return home or stay at their posts. Not like those of us working in Saffron's house.

The mistress and her family were seated in the middle of the platform, encased in the same robes the other Sovereign wore. Bastian had been roused especially for the gathering, but he looked as drunk as he had during dinner, all slouched over in his chair. The hood of his own robe was up, hiding his face from view, but I had no doubt that he either had his eyes closed or was at the very least struggling to keep them open.

At his father's side, Lysander wore a smirk that was visible even beneath his hood, and it made my skin feel as if I were crawling with the vermin that lived on the heads of the Fortis. I was unsure which was worse, the look of indifference on Saffron's face, or the utter glee on her son's.

The chairs they sat in were elaborate, carved from wood and ornate enough that they would look at home inside the dining room of Saffron's house, and more than ever before it struck me how wrong all of this was. That the Sovereign should have something so elaborate reserved for punishments while my people lived in huts and starved. How could these people not see how unfair they were being? How could they not understand why Ronan had tried to take the bread? How could I continue to stand back and do nothing?

Because I was powerless.

The murmur of voices echoing through the air died down when Saffron stood, and the long cape she wore swished around her as she walked to the front of the podium.

"Bring the boy," she called, her voice seeming to bounce off the walls of the surrounding buildings.

A door at my back opened with a boom that seemed as loud as a crack of thunder, and footsteps followed only seconds later. I could hear Ronan's quiet sobs, and as the sound grew closer, I found myself squeezing my eyes shut. They were still closed when the guards dragged the boy by me, but when the footsteps stopped and I heard a grunt that told me Ronan had been forced to his knees, I made myself open them. This was my doing, and ignoring what I had done would not take the blame from my shoulders.

"Ronan of the Outliers has been accused of theft," Saffron began, her voice ringing out louder than before, but still not loud enough to drown out Ronan's cries. "He has not only broken our laws, but betrayed our trust, and in order to make restitution for what he has done, he will face punishment."

Saffron nodded to the Fortis guard at Ronan's side before returning to her chair. At the front of the platform, the boy was forced onto his stomach by the very same guard that had been watching me for weeks. The one whose eyes I had mistakenly seen swimming with sympathy just hours ago. It took almost no effort for the man to hold Ronan down, but the guard still pressed his knee into the child's spine. The brutality of it filled me with a burning hate for this guard, this large man who could have held Ronan down with just one hand but instead chose to be rough. He was inhuman, just as all the other Fortis were. This child was no threat to them. Even if Ronan used all the strength inside him, he would be no match for the man at his back.

A second guard grabbed Ronan's left arm and stretched

it out to his side and forced the boy's palm flat against the ground. The man held the arm in place, and sweat beaded on my forehead. I watched in frozen horror as a third Fortis man stepped forward. The axe in his hand shone under the streetlights, and just the sight of it made me sway.

I had to do something. I had to stop this. How could I stand back and do nothing again? It was wrong. All of this was wrong. I had to stop it.

I stayed where I was, trembling but unable to move.

Ronan balled his hand into a fist and closed his eyes. He swallowed, and to his credit I could tell that he was working hard to stop from crying. He managed to get his sobs under control, but he must not have been strong enough to fight back the tears, because they ran down his cheeks in a never-ending stream.

The guard with the axe looked toward Saffron, who nodded again. Then the man raised the weapon, and for the second time the electric lights glinted off the blade. I found my own fingers curling into fists as the pounding of my heart echoed in my ears. My gaze was on Ronan, on his tear-streaked face, which was so scrunched up it looked as if he was already in pain. Even though my gaze was not focused on the man with the axe, I saw when he brought it down. My whole body jerked, but I was still focused on Ronan. Still staring at the child's terrified face.

The thud of the axe against the floor bounced off the walls of the surrounding buildings, echoing through the air. Ronan's eyes flew open and the tendons in his neck stretched taut, and then his mouth opened and a scream that would haunt me for the rest of my life ripped its way out of him. It seemed to slam into me, knocking the wind from my lungs and making my knees weak. I stumbled back and had to reach out to Mira to stop myself from falling. Her cheeks were streaked with tears when she looked at me, and it was the moment I saw them shimmering on her cheeks that I realized I was crying as well.

EIGHT

RONAN WAS DEAD WEIGHT AS I CARRIED HIM through the city. Mira had gone on ahead, leaving the second the gathering had ended so she could make it to the village and get help. The Sovereign doctor had stopped the bleeding and cauterized the wound to ensure that Ronan did not bleed to death on the way home, and had then given him a small vial of something to help with the pain. But that was it, and I knew Ronan could still die of shock or infection if he did not get help soon.

Isa walked at my side, sobbing. "Is he dead?"

"No," I huffed, shifting the boy so I had a better grip. I was lucky he was small for his age, especially since I was such a short person, but he was still not easy to carry. "He passed out. The pain was too much."

It had been more than three years since anyone had been caught stealing inside Sovereign City. Even then it had been an Outlier from another village, so I had not seen the results directly. But I had been told stories, we all had, Ronan included. Even without my warnings, he had known what he was risking when he took that bread, but he had done it anyway. Things with his family must have been worse than I realized.

We reached the gate and I was relieved when the Fortis in charge let us out without a fight. I stumbled as I passed through, and I found myself wishing that Ronan were awake enough to hold onto me, although I knew the wish was selfish. If he were awake, he would be in agonizing pain. The more time he spent unconscious, the better it would be for him.

With the sun down, the Fortis village was more rambunctious than usual, and the verbal abuse began only a beat after the gate banged shut behind me. The men and women who lived here hated us even more than the Sovereign did, a fact I had never stopped to wonder about before. At the moment though, their dislike of Outliers was more than just inconvenient—it would have been nice if someone here had offered to help me carry the boy home— but I suddenly realized that it made no sense. We were not to blame for their position in life, we were even worse off than they were, and yet they despised us and defended the Sovereign. Why? What had happened to make things this way?

A large man stepped from the crowd and blocked my way. "You're not going to make it very far with that boy, little girl."

"I will if you move out of my way," I managed to get out.

Isa looked at me with eyes that were twice as wide as usual, and it suddenly hit me what I had said and who I was talking to. Antagonizing this man would not help me—if anything, it would do the opposite—but the words had just slipped out. I worked hard to hold in the thoughts that popped into my head in and around the city, but at the moment I was exhausted, both emotionally and mentally, and I was ready to burst. It felt as if every emotion I had managed to keep in all day long was trying to erupt out of me, and this man, no matter how big and scary he was, seemed like the perfect target.

"What did you say?" he asked, narrowing his eyes on me.

He took a step closer, forcing me back. It was only a small step, but it was a small step in the opposite direction. Our village was the other way, through this mountain of a man, and I had to get Ronan out of here soon or he could die.

"Please," I managed to huff out. "I just need to get him home."

"And I need someone to take my aggression out on," the man said, his gaze moving to the girl at my side. "This one will do."

He made a move in Isa's direction and she slunk back until she was behind me, preventing me from making an escape. I was trapped between two children, Ronan in my arms, injured and out cold, Isa behind me, cowering in fear.

Even worse was the fact that I was no match for this man, not on my own, and not with two other people to worry about. There was nothing I could do.

"Isa," I said, "Can you take Ronan? Can you get him home?"

"W-what?" The girl's voice trembled its way out of her.

"You can take your aggression out on me." I turned and tried to hand Ronan off to Isa. "You have to get him home. Drag him if you need to, but do it. Mira should be at the village by now. They will meet you with a wagon, which means you only have to get Ronan that far. Not the whole way back. You can do it. Understand?"

Isa tried to take the boy from my arms, but she was thin and undernourished despite her height, and she lacked the strength to lift him. When he slipped from her grasp, I knew it was no use. She would never be able to get him home on her own.

I turned to face the man. "Do what you must, but be fast about it."

The man grabbed my arm, his fingers digging in and surely leaving bruises behind, and let out a loud bellow of a laugh. "Outliers are always in such a hurry."

"Let her go, Thorin."

My arm was still in the man's grasp when we both turned toward the voice. He materialized from the crowd, a broad frame that stood out even among other men. It was the guard from Saffron's house.

"What's it to you?" Thorin asked, tightening his grip on my arm until a whimper was forced out of me. "You have something going on with this Outlier, Asa?"

"No, but I'm not going to stand by and let you bully three kids," Asa replied.

I may have been small, but I was far from a kid. Not that I was in any position to argue the point. Not when Isa was sobbing behind me and Ronan was lying on the ground at my feet.

Asa grabbed Thorin's hand and physically pried my arm from his grasp. I stumbled back when I was free, pausing for only a beat to rub my sore forearm before dropping down at Ronan's side. He was still out, which made lifting him back into my arms twice as difficult, especially with my forearm throbbing the way it was. I would have a bruise for sure, but it was a small worry compared to what Ronan faced.

"Why do you care what happens to Outliers?" Thorin growled behind me.

"Because I'm not an animal, and neither are they." Asa turned his back on Thorin, putting his large frame between the Fortis man and us. "Let me help."

I tried to resist when he reached out to take Ronan from my arms, but just like with Thorin, it was impossible. This man was too strong, too big, too imposing to resist. In a beat he had the boy in his arms and had started walking, right by Thorin.

I grabbed Isa's hand and pulled her after Asa. All around us the men and women in the Fortis village had stopped to watch, but no one bothered to interfere. I was unsure why or whose side they were on, I just knew that this man, the very man who had held Ronan down only a short time ago, was helping us, and as much as I refused to be grateful, I was relieved.

I remained silent until the village was behind us and we had reached the point where the Lygan Cliffs began. "Stop. You helped, now let me have him back."

Asa continued walking. "I have him."

"Just like you had him when they cut his hand off?" I snapped, once again unable to rein in my emotions.

The Fortis man stopped walking and I did as well. Behind me Isa whimpered. Asa turned to face me, and when my gaze met his, I expected rage, hate even, but I was unprepared for what I saw swimming in his eyes. Pain. Grief. Regret.

"You know I had no choice," he said softly.

We stood face to face, him towering over me with Ronan in his arms and me a small Outlier who was totally at his mercy. I thought about all the times over the last few weeks when I had caught this man watching me. None of it made sense. Not the way he stared at me, not that he was helping me now. Not the fact that I found myself unable to keep quiet after years of discipline.

"I do have a choice," I told him, "and I choose to take Ronan and go back to my people alone. I do not want you there, and I can only imagine how he would feel if he woke and the first thing he had to see was the face of the very man who held him down while his hand was cut off. I have no doubt that your face will haunt his dreams enough without that." I closed the distance between us and tried to take Ronan from Asa the same way he had taken the boy from me, by force. When he resisted I said, "Make this easier on him. Do not torture him more than you already have."

Ronan's body slipped into my arms and Asa stepped back. The expression of shock he wore made it seem as if my words had genuinely wounded him. As if he actually cared about Ronan's pain, or even that he might carry some pain of his own over what he had done.

Good, I thought. *Let him suffer. Let him think about the things he has done and let them keep him up at night.*

"Come on, Isa," I called as I started walking again.

She scurried after me, and to my utter relief Asa stayed where he was.

With my arms full, I was unable to carry a knife, but I made sure we stopped so Isa could retrieve our weapons from under the rock. If we were attacked I would be forced to drop Ronan, but it was a risk we would have to take. It was the only way to get him home.

The boy felt twice as heavy as he had before, but thankfully he had been in my arms for only a short time when the sound of horse hooves echoed off the cliffs at my side. I slowed to a stop, so out of breath that I was unsure if I would have been able to go much further anyway, and a beat later the cart broke out of the darkness.

The moon shone down on the driver, glimmering off his blond curls. Bodhi was driving. Just the knowledge that I would very soon be able to hand my burden over to him made me move again. Even better, as the cart grew closer, I was able to make out the woman at his side. Adina.

A sob broke out of me when Bodhi pulled on the reins and the horse skittered to a stop. He and Adina were out of the cart in a blink, but it was not fast enough. I went down, falling to my knees with Ronan still in my arms.

"Indra." Bodhi dropped to the ground at my side.

"Take him," I gasped between sobs. "Help him."

Bodhi did as I asked, easing Ronan from my grasp. I had been dying to hand him off since the moment I scooped him into my arms, impatient to know that he was with Adina and would get help, but now that he was gone the loss felt as if a major part of me had been ripped away, and I found myself crying harder. I stayed where I was, unable to get to my feet and walk to the cart. All I could do was kneel on the cracked desert ground and cry as I relived the moment when Ronan's hand had been cut from his body. The scream he had let out, the blood that had soaked the floor, the look of agony on his face. I would never be able to banish the images from my mind. They were going to haunt me until the day I died.

"Indra." Bodhi was suddenly at my side again, kneeling, urging me to stand. "We have to go."

I allowed him to help me to my feet. That was when I realized that Isa was already in the cart, in the back with Ronan and Adina. They were waiting for me, but I was still dragging my feet. I knew we needed to go, to get Ronan home, but I felt like I was soaring above my body, looking down, and I could do nothing to make my legs obey.

"Indra." Bodhi continued calling my name.

"She is in shock," I heard Adina say from somewhere in the distance.

"I have you."

Bodhi scooped me up and moved, carrying me to the cart. He deposited me on the seat before hurrying around to the other side so he could climb in as well. Once he was there, he pulled me closer, careful to keep one arm around me as he clicked the reins. The horse moved, following Bodhi's prompting, and turned around so we could head back to the village. I stayed where I was, close to the man who thought I was perfect and wanted to take care of me for the rest of my life, suddenly wishing that I could just give in and let him.

Just before we turned I happened to look up. The moon was big and full, and just bright enough to illuminate Asa. He was a good distance away now, but he was still standing where I had left him, watching us drive away. Even from a distance the expression on his face told me that my words had found home in his heart, and despite my better judgment, despite the hatred I felt for the Fortis, guilt squeezed my insides.

"HOW ARE YOU FEELING?" BODHI ASKED AS HE knelt at my side. "You had me worried."

My mother was across the hut on her own bed, pretending to sleep in order to give us some privacy, but Anja was nowhere in sight.

"Adina says I was just in shock."

"I know, but at the time I had no idea what was going on, just that you were acting like a different person. Not the woman I know so well." Bodhi ran his hand over my head, brushing my hair back, and his touch was as soothing as ever. "You scared me."

"You already said that," I told him. "How is Ronan?"

"He will heal. Adina says he will have a lot of pain, but the medicine the Sovereign sent will help. He got lucky, all things considered."

"Yes," I muttered as my eyes filled with tears. "Lucky. We are all lucky that the Sovereign have allowed us to live. That they have decided they still need someone to clean up after them and to grope during dinner." My voice broke and I turned my face away when the tears forced their way from my eyes.

Bodhi pressed his face against mine, and when his hot breath brushed over my cheek, it warmed me more than a fire on a cold day. "Stop. Please. I cannot think about that happening to you. You have no idea what I want to do. I want to go to that city and find my way in and make them all suffer. I want—"

"No." I grasped his head, threading my fingers through his blond hair and pulling him closer. "Do not say that. You cannot even think it. They will kill you. Do you hear me? They will kill you."

Bodhi untangled himself from my grasp so he could see my face. His eyes searched mine, open and full of wonder. "Would you care?"

A lump formed in my throat that made it nearly impossible to talk. "Bodhi," I whispered.

His eyes searched mine for only a beat longer, and then his lips covered mine. We had never kissed before, but the moment our mouths met, I knew. Knew what he had known since we were five years old. There was a reason this man had refused to stop chasing me. It was because we belonged together, Bodhi and I. Because I loved him as much as he loved me. For too long I had let the Sovereign dictate my life. Had kept my emotions in check to keep me out of trouble, and the habit had followed me home, had forced me to ignore the feelings this man brought out in me.

Bodhi's lips slowed, but he kept them pressed against mine when he whispered. "Marry me, Indra. Marry me."

"Yes," I said, giving in and finally letting this man catch me.

NINE

THE JOYFUL MOOD IN MY HOME OVER THE NEWS that Bodhi and I were to be married contrasted with the somber one in Saffron's house. Ronan's theft had fueled the flames of Stateswoman Paizlee's party, and people were calling for reform. More regulations for the Outliers who came into the city, as well as better security before they left the walls. Outliers who had worked in Sovereign City for decades were looked at with suspicion, and in many cases wages were cut. We as a people were already struggling, and having our rations reduced any time was bad, but during the height of winter it was likely to be a death sentence for some. We could hunt, but we gathered, grew, and stored food based on need, and the sudden change meant that many families would go into the worst part of winter hungry.

To Saffron's credit, she kept our wages the same, but her attitude did change. She was stricter, something she said she felt bad about even as her eyes told a different story, and floggings became more common. Little things she had overlooked before were now punished, like a spot on a uniform or tracking dirt into the kitchen, both things that were nearly impossible to avoid in the middle of winter.

I did my best to keep my head down, but the mistress's opinion of me had changed as well. I had brought a thief into her house, had made her look like a fool in front of Stateswoman Paizlee, and as a result every little thing I did was picked apart by Saffron. If I poured too little wine into her glass she snapped at me, if I dripped even a tiny amount on the tablecloth it was five lashes. If I was too slow to bring the food, walked too fast while carrying her crystal goblets, did not talk loud enough when I answered her, or curtsy low enough. Nothing made Saffron happy anymore, which made Lysander happier than ever.

He had never forgiven me for refusing to allow him to get the best of me a second time, or that I had managed to protect Mira from him for all these years. I had learned my lesson about Lysander the hard way after working in Saffron's house for only one week, and had worked hard to protect my friend from the same fate. From the moment Mira set foot in the house, I had kept an eye on her, guided her on what to do and how to avoid Lysander, even putting myself in danger a few times when I was unsure if he was around. It had worked, and three years later Mira had only had to endure a cursory grope from him.

After what happened with Ronan, Asa kept his distance, but he continued to watch me. It was unnerving, knowing that he always kept me in his line of sight, and I was still unsure what his attentions meant or how they had come about. If he was hoping to catch me doing something wrong so I would get into trouble, or if he was watching my back. It felt like the latter, but *why* would he care? Why would a Fortis man be anything but indifferent to me, an Outlier?

It seemed that every day some poor Outlier found themselves in the stocks overnight, and passing them as I ran errands throughout the city made me physically sick. There was nothing I could do, but the knowledge was no comfort. Ignoring the suffering of my own people kept me up at night, but I was powerless to do anything about it. We all were.

Floggings had been rare before, but now there was at least one a week. Men, women, children, the age of the person was unimportant to the Sovereign. Anyone they thought was insolent or untrustworthy, whether or not they had proof, was punished. There were times when I could hear the screams from the town square the second I set foot inside the city, and it made me sick.

Coming home to my village every evening though, or more accurately to Bodhi, helped wash away the anguish that I felt over what was being done to our people. Our conditions were no better, there were still families who struggled to find enough food to eat, and we still had to defend ourselves against the dangers that lurked in the wilds, but the world seemed suddenly brighter to me. Things I had taken for granted for so long, such as the way the icy tree branches sparkled under the sun, were now breathtakingly beautiful.

Bodhi unashamedly met me at the edge of our village every day now, and seeing him felt like a reward for having to bear everything happening in the city. I savored his smiles and looks, and his warmth when he reached out to touch me. Just a brush of his fingers against my own made my insides flutter like the wings of a bird.

We spent evenings with his family, his parents and two brothers chattering away with an animated cheerfulness I was unused to since my own family was more reserved. Then we would go and sit with my mother, whose health seemed to have taken an upward jump since the news that Bodhi and I would get married. Anja would often join us, bringing Jax with her from time to time, and the quiet deference they showed one another told me that she would be very soon following me into marriage.

I felt as if everything was falling into place despite all the atrocities I saw in the city, and every night when I lay my head down to go to sleep, I found myself praying that it would continue. That I would be able to hold onto the happiness I had managed to catch.

But deep down, I knew that I was only an Outlier, and in this world, Outliers were undeserving of happiness.

THE BIGGEST CHANGE IN THE CITY CAME AS suddenly as a rainstorm in spring, and it happened only three weeks after Ronan's punishment.

It just so happened to be a day when Mira had been forced to stay home with a cold, which meant that not only had I made the long trek from the village unaccompanied, but also that I now found myself getting ready to leave Saffron's house alone. I never enjoyed the days when I had to travel through the borderland alone, but since Outlier shifts inside Saffron's house were scattered—ensuring that the family never had to lift a finger—no one else from the house was heading home at the same time as me.

Just as I turned toward the door after hanging up my apron for the day, Asa appeared in the mudroom, his hulking frame blocking the door from my view completely.

"New procedure," he said in an emotionless tone that made me think of Saffron.

I wanted to step back, to put space between myself and the man who had held Ronan down while his hand was cut off, but there was nowhere to go. Then another guard stepped into the room behind him and my heart began to pound faster, reminding me of the beat of drums that sometimes sounded through the wilds, coming from one of the other villages.

"What do you mean?" I whispered, unable to find any of the boldness that had come over me the day he helped carry Ronan through his village to the borderland. I told myself it had nothing to do with the pain I had seen in his eyes that day, but I knew it was a lie. Fortis or not, the knowledge that I had hurt this man affected me.

"There's a new law," the Fortis man at his side said. "It has been decreed that everyone will be stripped and searched before they leave the house. The Outliers cannot be trusted."

A shudder moved down my spine and I found it impossible to remain where I was. I stepped back, but it only took me deeper into the mudroom. Asa blocked the door that led outside while the other man, whose name was unknown to me, blocked my way to the kitchen. My gaze moved from one man to the other, stopping on Asa, but I found speech impossible. They had to be joking. Surely not even the Sovereign would demean us in such a way.

"What is he saying?" I managed to get out as I searched Asa's brown eyes for answers that I felt certain I did not want to hear.

"You are to be stripped and searched every day before you leave the house."

Something flickered in his eyes, an emotion I had seen only once before, on the day Ronan was punished, after Lysander had groped me in front of everyone. It was a mixture of sympathy and rage, and it made no sense. Not in this man's eyes. Not in the eyes of any Fortis man or woman.

"It's the law," he said, his voice much quieter this time, "and I'm charged with enforcing it. Do you wish to remove your own clothing or will I have to do it for you?"

Anger and shame heated my face as all the sympathy I felt for Asa slipped away. "You will not touch me," I hissed, feeling suddenly like a lygan right before it attacked.

I balled my hands into fists and glared at the man in front of me, wanting to hit him, to scream. Wanting to destroy this whole city and every person living in it.

Only it was impossible for me to do anything. I was nothing but an Outlier, and a woman on top of that, and I was no match for any man. Especially not a Fortis guard.

"I will do it if you make me." Asa paused and his eyes searched mine, and the pleading in them once again gave me a start. "*Don't* make me."

Despite my anger and confusion about the situation I currently found myself in, my voice was shaky when I said,

"This is wrong. You know it."

In my desperation, I found myself pleading with the man in front of me, begging him to help me the way he had that day three weeks ago. Except there was nothing he could do and I knew it. No matter how much I wanted to hate him for this, I knew he was powerless to stop this from happening. We all were.

"I'm only doing my job," Asa replied.

He was telling the truth, but I needed to direct my anger at someone, and the man in front of me was a convenient target, so I flung words at him that I knew would cut deep. I wanted them to, wanted them to hurt him as much as I was hurting now, as much as Ronan was still hurting.

"You can tell yourself that all you want, but it does not absolve you of the things you have done."

Asa visibly jerked at my words, but he held his ground. "I was born into this position just as you were born into yours. Do you have a choice in the things you do?" My anger waivered and began to sizzle out, and he saw it. "Neither do I." His eyes darted to the other guard, who stood silently watching me. "*Please.* Make this easy on both of us. Do as you're told."

I lifted my chin, and it was the only act of defiance I could muster. "I will do this, but make no mistake. It is *not* for you. It is for me."

I took a few steps back, putting more space between the two men and myself. Then I reached up and began to unbutton my dress.

Both men watched, but it was Asa that I focused on. Part of me wanted to focus on something else, to avoid looking into the brown eyes of this hulking man as I stripped myself bare for his inspection, but another part of me wanted to see his reaction. To know what he was thinking and feeling so I could understand him better and how exactly he fit into this world.

I kept my eyes on his even after I undid the last button and slipped the dress from my shoulders. The fabric slid down my body and dropped to the floor, pooling at my feet and leaving me in nothing but my undergarments. Heat flared across my cheeks and inside I was trembling with shame, but still I held his gaze.

Until now I had hated the silly undergarments Saffron forced upon us. The white fabric of the sleeveless shirt was thin, but it covered enough of my breasts that I tried to convince myself I was not naked. The skirt I wore under my uniform was made from the same material though, and when a shiver moved over my body, I found it impossible to hold onto the delusion.

Asa's eyes were still focused on mine when the other man said, "Remove everything."

A sob caught in my throat as Asa's gaze moved to the other guard. "She's fine. She can't hide anything under that."

The man scowled, but mercifully said nothing.

When Asa looked back at me, his gaze moved over my body for a beat before focusing on my face once again. He swallowed, and his Adam's apple bobbed, and then he said, "Raise your arms and turn."

I did as I was told, lifting my arms as I slowly spun in a circle. When I was facing him again, I captured his gaze with mine once more. The other guard stomped off, leaving us alone, and Asa finally looked away.

"I'm sorry," he said, nodding to the dress at my feet.

I swiped it up and held it against my chest. Looking at him was impossible, so I focused on the floor. "So am I."

For a beat neither one of us moved, and then he turned his back on me and walked from the room, leaving me to collapse on the floor.

I held my tears in this time, not like I had after Ronan's punishment, but instead sucked in mouthful after mouthful of air until the shame had melted away and I felt steadier. I had nothing to be ashamed of, I knew that, but it was easy to allow the sensation in. Only, I was unsure if Asa had anything to be ashamed of either. I knew just from looking him in the eye that he carried the shame of what he had done with him, but he was not at fault. He played no part in making the laws, and he did not hold others under his thumb, and he had even stopped me from having to strip down to nothing. It seemed that like me, Asa was just trying to survive. It was all either of us could do.

WHEN I HAD RE-DRESSED AND PULLED MYSELF together, I headed out. After what had happened in Saffron's house, I felt as if every person I passed on the street was staring at me. Other Outliers because they knew what had just happened and felt bad for me, the Fortis because they were wishing they had been in Asa's position, the Sovereign because they wanted to force me to strip down again. The once peaceful walk out of the city felt suddenly more treacherous than even passing the Lygan Cliffs did, and I was certain that if I did not get out of here soon, I would be attacked.

I practically ran through the streets, pushing people aside in my hurry to make it to the gate, but there was a line to get out, and it took only one glance in the direction of the gate to figure out what the hold up was.

The guards were taking advantage of the new law.

I watched in horror as an Outlier woman undid her dress and allowed it to drop to the ground, stripping in the middle of the street until she was in nothing but the thin undergarments. I had no doubt that she had been given a choice, and I knew why this was the route she had chosen. It was either strip in the street or the office, and we all knew what would happen in the office. It was not much of a choice, or at least that was what I thought, except that only a few moments later another Outlier woman followed a guard to the little room. Her head was down and her bottom lip trembled, but she went anyway. I found it impossible to understand how anyone could think what was going to happen in there was a better alternative to stripping down in the streets, but it was likely that she thought she could strike some kind of deal with the guards. Maybe she would be able to. Maybe sacrificing her body once would save her down the road. It was impossible to say.

Older men and women made it out of the city with no problem, but everyone else was treated to the same ultimatum. Woman after woman stripped for the male guards, but the Outlier men were no better off. While I watched, a Fortis woman forced a man to strip down to nothing, mocking his thin frame when he did. It was too much to handle, and I had to look away.

I knew I would be no different. I had already endured one strip, and I realized that as humiliated and angry as I had been, it was nothing compared to what could have happened to me. To what was about to happen. This would be a whole different level of humiliation. Suddenly, I understood what had actually occurred in Saffron's house, and the realization made me see Asa in a new light. He had planned the whole thing. He had put himself in that position to ensure that nothing too traumatic would happen to me. Asa got off work at the same time that I did. He could have walked away, could have turned his back on me and left me at the mercy of the other guards in the house, but he had made sure he was the one in that room. He had watched out for me.

For a reason that was impossible for me to comprehend, this man felt as if we had some connection, and whatever it was and wherever it had come from was unimportant, because it had saved me. He had spared me, and instead of being thankful, I had thrown words at him that were intended to sting. And I had hit the mark.

The closer I got to the front of the line, the more my body began to tremble. I knew what I had to do, I could not go into that room, but I had no idea how I would get through being stripped in the middle of the street, was unable to imagine how I would ever be able to hold my head up after this.

"Come on, girl," the guard barked when it was finally my turn.

I stepped forward on shaky legs and as steadily as I could muster replied, "I have already been searched by a guard working in the House of Saffron."

The man at the gate grabbed my forearm and jerked me forward. "I don't care. Strip."

My fingers were trembling when I reached up to unbutton my dress for the second time today. I had no choice. I just had to get it over with and pray that it went no further than my undergarments.

"Stop," a booming voice said from behind me, and even before I turned, I knew who had said it. Still, I found it nearly impossible to believe my eyes when Asa pushed his way through the crowd. "I searched this one already."

"New protocol," the guard in front of me barked.

Asa's back straightened and he met the cold stare of the other guard with one of his own. "I read the law, Idris, and I say she's already been stripped."

Idris pushed me aside so he could get in Asa's face and I stumbled back a couple steps, my fingers still on the button.

"Why are you always on the side of Outliers?" he growled.

"I'm on the side of the law," Asa hissed in reply.

There was a pause, and then Idris's top lip curled up in disgust. "Fine." He took a step back, his eyes still on Asa, and waved to me. "Go, girl. Before I change my mind."

My fingers redid the buttons on my dress while my legs carried me to the gate. Asa was at my side, walking as fast as I was. But I knew the gate would only protect him until Idris finished his shift. Then Asa would have to answer for what he had done here. For standing up for me. Again.

We made it through the gate before he grabbed my arm and pulled me through the village. The eyes of everyone we passed seemed to be on us and Asa's grip was neither gentle nor rough. He was frantic, rushed. Like he was desperate to get me to safety.

His pace remained steady until we had left the village behind, and when he finally came to a stop, I was pretty sure it was the same spot I had left him in only three weeks earlier when I had ripped Ronan from his grasp.

Asa let go of my arm and his hand dropped to his side. "I'm sorry."

"I can tell," I said, looking up into his dark eyes, trying to see inside him and understand what was going on with this man. "Why? Why do you care what happens to me?"

"Because you're a person. Like me."

I looked beyond him, back toward the village we had just fled. "How many other people in your village feel that way? Not many I bet."

"I only have to answer for how I feel."

His words filled me with awe, and I dragged my gaze from his village so I could look at him again, whispering, "Thank you."

Asa's gaze moved to the dry ground beneath our feet as if he found it impossible to look me in the eye. "Don't thank me. I forced you to take your clothes off. I degraded both of us."

"You did it so no one else would," I said, acknowledging the truth of the situation out loud.

"The other men in the house..." His eyes were still on the ground when he exhaled. "It's wrong."

"I have worked in that house for three years. Why do you suddenly care what happens to me?"

"I've always cared what happened to you." His eyes flickered up, focusing on mine for only a moment before going back to the ground. "You just never noticed until now."

A beat after the words passed his lips, he turned. I watched dumbfounded as he headed back to his village, leaving me standing in the street alone, just as I had done to him three weeks earlier.

TEN

THAT NIGHT IN MY VILLAGE, JUST AS THE SUN was
setting over the wilds, Bodhi and I were married.

I made the decision to not tell him—or anyone
else—what had happened to me inside the walls of Sovereign
City. It would have been easy to say I did it to protect him
from his own anger, or even because I did not want anyone
to have to share in my pain, but the humiliation I felt over the
experience told me those excuses would have been a lie. No, I
refused to run the risk of Bodhi going into the Fortis village
in search of revenge, and I hated thinking about what would
happen if he made trouble with the Sovereign, but I also
burned with shame at the memory of having to strip down
for Asa and the other guard. It was unfair, the decision had
not been mine, but I still *felt* as if I were somehow to blame.
As if I could have done something to stop it from happening,
not just to me, but to all the other Outlier women who had

been stripped bare under the pretense of being searched. Because that was what this new law was. A pretense. The Sovereign in charge, women like Paizlee, did this to exert their power over us, to ensure that the Outliers were thoroughly put in their place. Worst of all, it worked.

As for the Fortis, like the guards at the gate, they were playing a different kind of game. One that made them strong and us weak, a game that they had been playing with the Outliers for as long as I could remember. Probably for as long as anyone could remember, and even beyond that.

It was because of these things that Bodhi and I started our marriage with a cloud hanging over us. One that was invisible to him, but one that I was certain he could sense. He asked no questions, just as he had not asked me about most of the things that had happened inside the walls for the past three years, but I could tell by the way he touched me, by the gentle caress of his fingers when he took my hand in front of our entire village, that he knew I needed our life to be a refuge from the atrocities I saw every day inside the walls. That I needed *him* to be my safe haven. I also knew that if anyone in my life could be that for me, it was Bodhi.

The ceremony was short, just Bodhi and me holding hands in front of the village and vowing to commit our lives to one another, and then receiving the passage markings that indicated we were now one. I had attended dozens of marriages during my lifetime, but never before had I thought about the markings married couples wore or what they really symbolized. Sitting at Bodhi's side though, watching as his father used the tebori tool to etch the markings onto my new husband's skin, I was overwhelmed by how beautifully significant this ceremony was.

His father began by carving the passage markings on Bodhi's temples that indicated his son was now the head of his own household, which consisted of a half circle with another closed circle in the middle. When he had finished those, he moved the tool to his son's forehead and began the markings that both Bodhi and I would receive, the ones that symbolized we were now husband and wife. I held my breath and watched it happen, feeling each tap of the tebori against his skin as if the very same lines were being carved on my heart. When the marks on Bodhi's head were complete, his father took the bowl of black dye, made from a small beetle common in the wilds, and rubbed it into the scratches, revealing the design he had created. The result was beautiful. A single tear drop with two dots above it and lines extending from both sides, each one ending in another dot.

Then it was my turn, and Bodhi held my hand as his father repeated the process on me, tapping the tebori tool against my forehead over and over again in the same pattern he had just completed on his son. Just like before, it felt as if the painful pricks sank into me, as if they wrapped around my heart and added an extra cushion that would protect me from the rest of the world, and the thought made me feel suddenly stronger.

After we had both received our new passage markings, Bodhi and I were presented to the village. We stood in front of everyone, holding hands as we swore to be eternally faithful to one another. It was a promise the Winta took very seriously, one that would haunt us in the afterlife if we broke it, and there was not a single doubt clouding my heart or mind as I repeated the words.

When the ceremony was over, Bodhi and I retired to our new hut, a gift from the elders in our village. Then we were finally alone.

I was not ignorant in the ways of sex, I had been made brutally aware of every detail three years ago as a new employee in the House of Saffron, but it was something Bodhi and I had not yet participated in. Every Outlier tribe was different, but the Winta believed that the joining of a man and woman was a sacred act, one that if not preformed correctly could curse a person's future. I had been happy to wait, and not just because it was our custom. Bodhi was not Lysander and I knew it would be different with him, but the memory of that day three years ago still caused me to tremble from time to time. Still made me hesitate.

The first night in our new hut, Bodhi succeeded in doing something no one else could: he managed to wipe every memory of Lysander from my mind. With my husband every touch was gentle, every caress a symbol of how much he cared for me, every kiss an act that went much deeper than even love. He wrapped me in his comfort, showed me not only how it was supposed to be between a man and a woman, but also how two people could complete each other so thoroughly.

For me, Bodhi had always been the antithesis of everything that was bad, even during all the years when I had run from him, but on our first night as husband and wife, he showed me just how much more he could be. He proved to me that even in the midst of the poverty and hopelessness that often stained our existence as Outliers, we could have a life that was full and wonderful because we had each other.

Afterward, as he held me in his arms, his grip somehow firm but not suffocating, he whispered, "I love you, Indra."

"I love you," I said as I looked up at him in awe, wondering why I had ever run from this man.

THE NEXT MORNING DURING OUR HIKE THROUGH the borderland, I told Mira about the new law and what had happened the day before with Asa.

"He helped you?" My friend's expression mirrored my own confusion when she looked my way.

"He did, and it was not the first time. The day Ronan was punished the same guard helped me get out of his village when I was cornered by another man. He even carried Ronan. I cannot begin to understand why he did any of these things, but I believe we can trust this man."

"He is the one who held Ronan down, Indra." When Mira shook her head, some of her blond curls escaped the bun sitting on top of her head and she was forced to shove them back in their home. "No. He is a Fortis. They are all the same."

"I believe Asa has genuine guilt over what he had to do, and that he is trying to make amends for it."

I also thought that this man, this Fortis guard who had been working in the same house as me for the past three years, had developed feelings for me somewhere along the way. When or why or how was a mystery, but it was obvious that because of these feelings, he was willing to look out for me. Bodhi was my husband and I had spoken the truth when I vowed to love only him for the rest of my life, but even if I had been lying, Asa would always be a Fortis and I would always be an Outlier. There was no possible future for two people from such different worlds. Something he had to know.

"He has a lot to make up for," Mira said.

Maybe she was right, or maybe the guilt he carried with him was no different than my own.

On an average day in Saffron's house, the path of the Fortis guards and Outlier servants rarely crossed. Typically only at mealtime, large celebrations included. During normal times they were rare, but with the approach of Lysander's wedding, these large gatherings had become more and more frequent. Saffron was hosting parties on a regular basis in order to celebrate the new couple, but she would also have people over to discuss the planning of the event. Then there were the dinners hosted for Paizlee's political connections. For Saffron's part it was done in hopes of smoothing over the problem I had created by bringing Ronan into the city, something the stateswoman had to be well aware of, but the two women had never gotten along, and even the impending marriage of their children was not enough to bridge the gap now.

But despite our conflicting schedules, it just so happened that Asa and I crossed paths very early in the day. Whether it was by his design or coincidence I was uncertain, but I had to admit that after yesterday and my discussion with Mira on the way to work, I was relieved to bump into him so soon after arriving at the house. The laws in Sovereign City were going to make life even more difficult for Outliers, but since the Sovereign placed the burden of enforcing these laws on the Fortis, Asa could be an asset to me—and to Mira. If this man really was determined to protect me, I would let him. Which was why I met his gaze head-on when we came upon one another in the hall outside the servant's bathroom.

The expression of surprise that crossed Asa's face was understandable, but it was gone in a moment, and then he looked around before saying, "I'll find you when your shift is over. I'll protect you."

"And Mira," I said. "My friend."

Asa hesitated, but it was only for a beat before his head bobbed in assent. "Okay."

He was a tall man, quite a bit taller than Bodhi and much broader, and standing so close to him in the hallway with no one else around, I suddenly felt his size more than ever before. Felt the vastness of his presence. Fear rippled through me at the thought of what this man could do to me and exactly how much trust I was putting in a total stranger.

"Why?" I asked in a whisper that was barely audible, even in such close proximity.

"You already asked me that," he replied. "Yesterday."

"But I am asking again, because I cannot understand. I cannot come up with an explanation for why a Fortis would care about an Outlier. Why you seem to care about *me* so much."

"Because you're better than the others," Asa said, bringing to mind the words Bodhi had said to me not that long ago. "I see it in how you look out for your friends. In how much you care about the other people in the house."

"It is what we do. We are Outliers. If we do not look out for one another, bad things can happen."

"It's more than that," Asa said. "You care more than the others. You can't see it, but I can." He hesitated, pausing as if trying to decide if he should say something or keep it to himself, then said, "I know what Lysander does. What he did to you."

I took a step back, putting more distance between us. The mention of Lysander made me shiver. Made me want to run and hide. But it also filled me with shame, as if I were at fault for what had happened.

"He has done it to everyone." I kept my gaze averted when I said it.

"Not to your friend. Mira?" He paused again, waiting for me to nod. "I know that you've kept her safe since she arrived. I know that you were the only one willing to speak up for the boy, Ronan. You are better, Indra, and I don't want that taken from you."

Until coming to work in Saffron's house, I had never been around electricity. That first day, after dinner was finished, I had tried to plug the vacuum in while my hands were still damp from washing the dishes. The jolt that shot up my arm had nearly knocked me on the floor. That was how I felt now. Hearing my name on Asa's lips was as shocking as that jolt of electricity had been.

"You know my name," I whispered.

"I do," he said in response, so quiet that it felt like a breeze had swept down the hall.

His gaze moved over me, but there was nothing predatory in it. It was simply a searching look, like he was trying to reassure himself that I was all right. When his eyes focused on the new passage markings on my forehead, I found myself reaching up to touch them. Not to cover them, I had no desire to hide the fact that I was bound to Bodhi, but to make sure the man in front of me understood the significance.

"You're married," Asa said.

It was not a question, but I nodded anyway. "I got married last night."

"He is a lucky man." Asa was the one who stepped back this time, as if the news that I was now a married woman made him want to put more space between us. "I'll see you at the end of your shift, Indra."

Then he turned and walked away, leaving me alone in the hall.

ELEVEN

T HE REST OF THE WORKDAY PASSED IN AN
unremarkable way, which was all I could really ask for
anymore. Saffron was too busy with Lysander's
upcoming wedding to give any of us more than a passing
moment of abuse, and her son was nowhere to be found.
Thankfully.

It was what I looked forward to the most about his
marriage, the fact that he would no longer be living under
this roof. Expanding inside the walls of the city was
impossible, meaning Lysander and his new wife would not
be able to have a house of their own, and in a society run by
women, it was tradition for the newly married couple to
move in with the wife's family. Meaning that after the
wedding, Lysander would be Paizlee's problem. I doubted
she would put any more effort into stopping his behavior
than his mother had, and I felt for the Outliers working in

that house, but I would have been lying if I said I felt no relief when I thought about him moving out. He was one problem that was about to take care of itself.

As the end of the workday drew near, I found myself feeling as uncertain as I had on my first day in Saffron's house. Back then things had been so uncertain that my mind felt as if it were overflowing with the many warnings and instructions my mother had tried to hammer in over the years. Only now all the worry inside me revolved around one thing: Asa and whether or not he was in fact a man of honor. He had seemed sincere during our few conversations, but Mira was right. He was still a Fortis, and they were as known for their dislike of Outliers as they were for their size and strength.

It seemed as if Mira carried the same worries with her, so much so that when our shift finally came to an end, she dragged her feet instead of hurrying to make her escape the way she usually did. I knew why, but I also felt certain that Asa would be waiting for us in the mudroom. With him, we at least stood a chance. With the other guards, there was none.

"We have to go," I told Mira when she moved to put away the dishes that sat drying on the counter, a job that belonged to the evening staff.

Mira nodded, but still made no move to head for the door.

"Mira." I grabbed her arm and forced her to turn and face me. "We need to go. Asa is waiting."

She jerked away as if I had hit her. "Asa?"

"That is his name."

"Are you friends with him now? With a Fortis? What would Bodhi say?"

"Do not bring him into this," I snapped, half in defense of my actions and half because I was terrified that she would tell him. Not afraid of Bodhi, but afraid *for* him. Afraid of what he would do if he knew everything happening in the city. "He would want me to take this opportunity if I could."

Mira's expression was hard, but I knew her anger was directed at the situation more than me. Not that it stopped her from giving me a fiery look when I pulled her toward the mudroom.

Just as he had promised, Asa was already waiting for us. Only this time he was alone.

"I've been waiting." He let out a breath that reminded me of just how much he was risking by doing this.

There was something else there too, though. Concern. The emotion was so clear that even Mira was unable to miss it, and under my grasp, I felt some of the tension melt from her body.

"Sorry for our tardiness," I said.

Asa's head bobbed once as his gaze moved to Mira, but it was only for a beat before he was once again focused on me. His brown eyes were soft, still swimming with worry, but with something else as well. Something I had only seen in one other person's eyes — at least when they were focused on me. Bodhi. Asa was looking at me the exact same way my husband did. As if he would be willing to do anything for me. Kill for me. Maybe even die for me. It was unnerving, but even worse was the fact that I could tell by the expression on Mira's face that she saw it too.

Asa tore his gaze from mine and focused on something behind me, back toward the now closed door that led from the mudroom into the kitchen. "We should go."

"Go?" Mira said, and the word rang with the same surprise shooting through me.

"Yes." Asa kept his gaze down when he turned toward the door.

"What about searching us?" Mira asked.

This time, he did glance over his shoulder, but his brown eyes focused on her, not me. "I won't do that. Not when no one else is here. But don't worry, if anyone asks I'll say it was done. I won't let anything happen to you."

Gratitude flooded my body at the unexpected turn of events, but it was followed quickly by guilt. Asa may not have been an Outlier, but he was not exempt from the laws the Sovereign set forth. He was risking everything for us, for me, and if he was caught, he would face punishment as surely as Mira and I would. Only it would be worse for him, because he would have to face the wrath of his people as well. People who hated us.

I was taking advantage of him, of his feelings for me. Refusing his help was impossible, I needed it for Mira's sake if not my own, but it still felt *wrong*. It was as if I was using his weakness to my advantage, and it was a position I was uncomfortable with.

"I am married," I said, drawing the gazes of both people my way. "You know that."

Asa's head dipped once in acknowledgement before he turned away again. "That's not what this is about."

Before I had a chance to even consider what else his help

could mean, the door was open and Asa had stepped outside.

I could feel Mira's gaze on me, but I refused to look at her and instead followed Asa out the door. She trailed after me, falling into step at my side only a few paces later, and we walked side by side through the city in silence. Asa stayed in front of us the entire way to the gate, but we maintained our distance to avoid drawing the attention of anyone we passed. Still, I felt as if everyone was watching us. As if they all knew what we were up to and were waiting to catch us so they could drag us to the city square for punishment.

We reached the gate and were greeted by the same sight as the day before, Outliers stripping down, the guards doing everything in their power to take advantage of the situation. At my side, Mira trembled and moved closer to me as we waited for our turn. Asa had fallen back so that he was now behind us, and clumped into a group the way we were, he did not bother keeping his distance. I could feel his presence as surely as I could feel Mira's hand wrapped around mine. Felt his size and strength just like I had in the hall today at Saffron's house. Only it no longer intimidated me. It comforted me.

The scene that played out when we finally reached the gate was an echo of the one from the previous day, only this time I neither argued nor made a move to unbutton my dress because Asa was already there. He stopped the guards from forcing us to strip, and then he made sure we got out of the city safely and through his village after that. With each step Mira relaxed even more, and when we finally stopped next to the rock that concealed our weapons, she turned and looked up at Asa with a mixture of wonder and gratitude on her face.

"Thank you," she said after a beat of silence.

Asa dipped his head in a nod, something I had noticed that he did quite often, and then looked away. It was almost as if the attention made him uncomfortable. "I'll do the same for you tomorrow."

His eyes flickered toward me, but they were focused on my forehead again. The passage markings seemed to warm under his gaze, reminding me of how it had felt only last night when Bodhi's father had etched them into my skin.

"Your husband watches out for you in your village?"

"He does," I replied.

This time when Asa nodded, his eyes remained down. "Good. I will watch out for you here."

Then, without another glance or word or indication of what he was thinking, he turned his back on us and walked away.

Mira and I watched him for only a beat before collecting our weapons and heading for home. We walked for some time in silence, each of us too lost in our thoughts to say much at first. I was puzzling over Asa still. He was a mystery, one I doubted I would ever be able to unravel, but one I was grateful for all the same.

"He is in love with you," Mira finally said.

The statement warmed my cheeks even though I had already come to this conclusion. "I know."

"And you?" She glanced my way, not turning her head completely when she did it, as if she thought it would make me more likely to answer her honestly. As if she thought I was hiding something from her. "Do you love him?"

"I know nothing about him, but the answer would be no either way. I love Bodhi. I would not have married him otherwise. Plus, no matter what Asa does to help me, an Outlier cannot be with a Fortis. It is impossible."

"Why?" Mira asked.

I turned my body to face her, walking sideways so that my back was to the Lygan Cliffs even though I had been taught to never lose my focus in this way. "Because we are not the same."

"Now you sound like one of the Sovereign." Mira's blue eyes rolled in their sockets, but her lips pulled up into a smile that helped to ease some of the sting her words had brought to me. "We are the same, Indra. We are all people. We have just been trained to believe that we are different."

I opened my mouth to argue with her, but no words came out. She was right. Sovereign, Outlier, Fortis, we were all just people. The only things that kept us apart were the walls that had been constructed years ago, both the physical ones and the ones that existed only in our minds. Those were built on oppression and prejudices so old that no one alive today had a clue why they even existed.

A click echoed off the rocks at my back, followed closely by a few more. In front of me, my friend's body went rigid. I spun to face the cliffs, the knife in my hand up and ready as more clicking rang through the air. But there was nothing in sight. Not yet, anyway.

"Where is it?" Mira hissed.

At my side, she too had her knife up. This was a position we had been in before, and as long as there was only one of the creatures, we knew what to do to defend ourselves. The problem would come if they were hunting in a pack. One lygan was dangerous enough, but four or five? Beating that many would be impossible.

We remained still. The clicks grew closer together and louder, but with the way the sounds echoed off the rocks, it was impossible to tell how many there were until the creature — or creatures — decided to show themselves.

"Be ready," I said for my benefit as much as for hers.

The hiss came first. It was a sound that was low and seemed to come from the deepest part of the animal's belly, and it was followed only a beat later by the appearance of the lygan itself. The creature was bigger than average, its tail as long as my arm and its body only a little shorter. Its claws clicked across the rocks as it scurried forward, seeming to move at an impossibly fast speed considering its stunted legs. The red and purple scales shone even in the limited light of the evening as the lygan twisted between the sharp rocks that made up the cliffs. Now that it was closer, the click of its claws seemed twice as loud, and when it hissed a second time, the sharp points of its teeth were visible.

Readying myself for a fight, I planted my feet. I knew from experience that the creature would pounce without warning, that was how Mira had been injured before, and I was ready when it finally flew through the air, headed right for me.

I slashed my knife up and the blade hit home on the lygan's stomach. It screeched just before its body slammed into mine, and when I flew back a cry retched from my body. We went down together, my back slamming into the dry ground and the lygan landing on top of me. It was injured and my knife was still in its belly, but it had not given up yet. The animal wiggled and snapped its jaw, and its teeth came close enough to my nose that I felt its moist breath against my face. Its yellow eyes were focused on me, the black pupils contracted to slits. The scales were smooth against my hand when I grabbed its neck in an attempt to hold it back, and its claws scratched at my body as it tried to get the advantage.

"Indra!"

Mira's voice seemed far away, but I knew she was nearby and ready to help. Just as I had been with her the day she was attacked. Her face appeared above me. The setting sun shone down on her blond hair, making it glow, and in the brilliant light her passage markings seemed twice as dark against her pale skin.

The sun reflected off the metal when she raised her knife and I had to turn my head away. My hand was still on the lygan's neck, holding the thing back as it snapped its teeth, but even before Mira had stabbed it I could feel its strength waning. Then she did, and when the knife entered the lygan's body, the creature let out a shriek that left a ringing behind in my ears. The lygan jerked and its claws clamped down on my stomach, puncturing my dress and forcing a scream out of me. Mira pulled her knife from the creature and brought it down again, and this time the animal let out a drained wail that was preceded by its entire body going slack.

When that happened, its claws relaxed as well, freeing me from the piercing hold it had on my body. I shoved the animal off and it rolled to the ground at my side. Mira was panting, as was I, and for a beat neither one of us moved. She stayed frozen, standing over me while I remained on my back, staring up at her.

Mira snapped out of it all at once, and then she was on her knees at my side. "Are you hurt?"

I shook my head even as I looked down to inspect my sides. Even though the claws had felt as if they were piercing my skin, they had barely punctured the fabric of my dress and there was no blood. The lygan had only been holding onto me.

"I am okay," I said, as surprised by the statement as Mira was.

When she nodded, some of her hair escaped the bun Saffron forced on us and fell around her face. "Stand up."

Mira held her hand out and I took it gratefully. My legs were shaky, but I was whole and the lygan was dead, and even if Saffron docked my wages to pay for a new uniform, I was grateful just to be alive.

My gaze moved to the lygan, now motionless on the ground. "We should take it home with us."

Mira exhaled as she worked to shove the loose tendrils of her hair back into its bun. "It will make a good stew."

"Yes," I said. "It will."

TWELVE

W E WORKED TOGETHER TO DRAG THE DEAD lygan through the borderland to the wilds. Back in our village, Mira took the carcass home to the hut she shared with her parents and younger brother. Bodhi had spent the day hunting, and I was confident that when I arrived home not only would he have a skinned animal cooking over the fire, but he would have also taken some of the meat to my mother and Anja. That was one aspect of life I no longer had to worry about now that Bodhi was my husband: meat. He was the best hunter in the village, always out early before the sun had risen and never returning home without something to show for his efforts, and thanks to him, my mother was getting stronger every day.

The scent of roasted meat met me when I stepped through the door of our hut, along with a smile from Bodhi, and the very sight of him was enough to push every other thought from my head. At least until his gaze moved down and the smile slipped from his lips.

My dress had holes in it from my altercation with the lygan, and there were even a few spots of blood on the skirt. I was certain that the rest of me looked no better.

Before Bodhi's imagination had time to conjure up another explanation for my disheveled state, I said, "Mira and I had to kill a lygan."

After what had happened inside the city, I was grateful to have something else to talk to Bodhi about, something that would distract him from the subject of the Sovereign. I had no desire to lie to my husband, but telling him what was going on inside the city would do nothing for either one of us. It was better to leave the city behind me when I left the walls. I had worked hard over the last three years to keep the different parts of my life in neat little sections of my brain, putting Sovereign City in a part that remained closed when I was home. Not only the bad things ended up there either. Asa also existed in that section. Good or bad, he was not an Outlier and had no business in my village.

"You killed it?" Bodhi asked.

"We did."

My husband smiled, and there was more than just relief in his eyes. There was pride as well. "I remember taking you into the forest when we were kids. Teaching you to shoot a bow."

"I remember you getting in trouble for that," I replied as

I worked to remove my hair from the knot twisted on top of my head.

"It is a foolish notion that women are weaker than men. It is only that way because we refuse to teach them to do things for themselves." He paused when my hair fell down around my shoulders in dark waves and pressed his lips together thoughtfully. "Tomorrow is your day off. I want to take you somewhere. A surprise."

"A surprise?" When I raised my eyebrows, the skin on my forehead stung, reminding me of the fresh passage markings, and oddly enough, of the way Asa had stared at them today.

"Yes." Bodhi planted a kiss on my nose. "Change out of that ridiculous dress so we can eat and head out."

When I undid the first button on my uniform, my mind was still mulling over the events of the day and the Fortis man who had helped me. Bodhi's eyes followed my every move, and the expression in them pushed all thought of Asa and Sovereign City from my mind. I pulled the dress over my head and the undergarments quickly followed, leaving me bare to my husband. He stepped closer, and the hunger in his blue eyes was unmistakable.

"Are you sure you want to leave the hut?" I asked him, eyebrows raised again despite the throb in my forehead.

"I am reconsidering," Bodhi said as he grabbed my hips.

He pulled my body flush with his, his grip firm but gentle, and the feel of his big hands on my hips sent a shiver shooting through me. Compared to the Fortis men who worked in Saffron's house, Bodhi was small, but I was a small person as well, and he was still much bigger than me.

So much so that I knew he could dominate me if he wanted to. But I also knew my husband would never do that, and it was this knowledge that made his size welcome. It made me see his overwhelming strength not as a threat, but as something for me to lean on. Something that would keep me safe. Forever.

Bodhi's mouth covered mine and he ran his hands up my back. Our lips moved together in a dance that felt more natural than anything I had ever done, and more thrilling, and not for the first time, I wondered why I had run from this man for so long.

"Indra." He whispered my name as he kissed his way down my neck. "I love you."

"I love you," I said, pulling at his shirt.

Bodhi helped me, removing the animal hide that covered his chest and tossing it to the ground. Then his mouth was on mine again and we were walking, kissing as we moved toward the bed. When we fell it was in a tangled mess of arms and legs, and all thoughts of leaving the hut were forgotten, all fears from the day too. There was nothing but Bodhi and me. Nothing but the feeling of his body against mine, and the knowledge that as long as he was with me, I would be safe and taken care of.

"DID I RUIN YOUR SURPRISE?" I ASKED BODHI, WHO was lying on the bed next to me.

He rolled onto his side and planted a kiss on my nose. "No. We can still go."

Bodhi heaved himself off the bed, but I remained where I was, watching as he gathered his discarded clothes. Unlike some of the other Outlier tribes, the Winta restricted our passage markings to our faces, leaving Bodhi's back and arms and chest untouched, but not unmarked. He had picked up scars over the last twenty-five years. A long one on his stomach from an altercation with a forest cat, and another on his left shoulder blade thanks to a close encounter with a rawlin, one of the bright red birds that inhabited the wilds. They had sharp beaks and sharper talons, and even though they usually steered clear of people, they had been known to attack. Especially if they happened to be hunting the same prey. There were other marks on Bodhi's body as well, each of them representing how hard he had worked to stay alive, and to me they also seemed to illustrate just how capable he was of being the provider and protector the men of the Winta tribe were supposed to be.

Bodhi was lean compared to the Fortis, although that could be said of all the Outliers, but he was still muscular. He worked to survive, as we all did, but he had no need for the brute strength the guards possessed. All Bodhi needed was to be healthy and fit, and the result was beautiful.

I was still lying on our bed with the fur pulled up to my chin, admiring my husband, when he finished dressing and turned to face me. He had a bag made of animal hides in his hand and a grin on his face that seemed to take root in my stomach and grow until it had wrapped its branches around my heart.

"You know that I enjoy seeing you with nothing on, but I think you should get dressed. It is cold."

I returned his smile. "I am getting up."

Somehow, having Bodhi stare down at my body as I lay bare before him made me feel like a different person. As if the woman that worked inside the walls was someone whose memories I had somehow obtained, not earned, and I loved my husband more than ever for that feeling. For making me feel new and whole once again.

I dressed, and together we left our hut. The snow that had fallen on our village had been packed down by feet and melted by the fires, leaving the ground between our huts damp and muddy. Winter in the wilds was short though, and before long the sun would grow too hot to maintain the snow at all. When spring came, life would be easier for all of us, but it too would be short-lived. Most of the year was taken up by summer, and the days were long and hot and the sun stifling. Once it arrived, my walk to and from Sovereign City would feel twice as long. Things would improve when I reached Saffron's house since the Sovereign had the ability to cool the air in their homes, a feat that still baffled me, but the scorching walk beside the wastelands was impossible to avoid, and already I was dreading the return of the heat.

Bodhi and I had just reached the center of the village when Isa came running up, and the grin she wore on her face was a welcome sight. Something in her had changed after Ronan's punishment, and since that day she had been more melancholy and silent when we were in the city. I checked on the boy often and had marveled at how well he was adjusting, but also at how he had managed to keep his spirits up. The same could not be said of Isa, though. It was almost as if she were the one whose hand had been taken that day.

"Indra, Bodhi!" She was out of breath when she stopped in front of us, but her smile remained.

"Are you alright?" Bodhi asked, grinning even though I knew his question was not rhetorical.

"Emori had her baby," Isa beamed. "A girl!"

My stomach felt as if it had fallen off a cliff, and my smile almost followed its descent. I had to force my mouth to stay stretched across my face. Isa was young, too young to understand what had happened between her sister and Lysander, and the last thing I wanted to do was scare her. Especially since she now worked in Emori's place.

"How is she feeling?" It was all I could think to say. Knowing what I did, it was impossible for me to congratulate Isa. The child was not at fault and I had no idea how Emori felt about the baby, but I knew too much to be happy myself.

"Good." Isa nodded her head so fast that her dark hair, which was pulled into a tail at the back of her head, bobbed back and forth. "And Xandra had a baby today too."

"Xandra?" I exchanged a look with Bodhi, but he seemed as confused as I was.

Like me, Xandra worked in Sovereign City, but we were on different shifts so it was rare that our paths crossed. It had been weeks, maybe longer, but the last time I saw her she had not looked pregnant. Plus, Xandra, although older than me, was still unmarried. It was not unheard of for a baby to be born this way, but it was rare, and usually the mother found herself in Emori's position. As Winta, we were held to a very strict moral code, and the risk of cursing your future marriage and taking the shame with you into the afterlife was a good deterrent. If Xandra had been with child, I was certain that someone would have mentioned it to me. Anja or my mother especially.

"Yes." Isa's tail bobbed again, and a second later she was darting past us, calling out, "I have to go!"

When she had disappeared between two huts, I turned to Bodhi. He saw more of the village than I did. Perhaps he knew what was going on.

"Was Xandra with child?"

Just as I had expected, he shook his head. "She was not."

"Where did the baby come from?"

The sun was already going down and Bodhi had said that he wanted to get me to his surprise before it got too dark, but curiosity got the better of us and we headed into the village instead of away from it. The hut Emori shared with her mother and Isa—and now the baby—was near Xandra's, and the closer we got, the more commotion could be heard. I was in no hurry to see the baby Lysander had forced upon Emori, but since I wanted to know what was happening with Xandra, I had no choice.

The area around their huts was thick with people though, making it impossible for us to get close enough to see either woman or baby. Instead, Bodhi and I found ourselves at the back of a large crowd that was excitedly waiting to see the new additions.

"Maybe we should go," he said.

Despite the fact that I was shorter than most of the adults in the village, I lifted myself up on my toes in an attempt to see over the heads of those around me. Suddenly the crowd parted and Adina materialized, forcing me to stumble back.

"Indra." The older woman grabbed my arm to stop me

from falling. "I did not see you."

"It is fine, you were just the person I wanted to see." It was untrue, but now that she was in front of me I was relieved to be able to get some answers without having to see Emori and her baby. "Isa told us that Xandra had a baby."

Adina's eyebrows jumped up, pushing the markings on her forehead with them. "Isa is wrong. Xandra brought a baby home with her."

"From where?" Bodhi asked.

"From Sovereign City."

Her explanation made no sense, and the only thing I could come up with was that Xandra had somehow stolen this baby from the city. That she had managed to smuggle the child out while the guards were occupied with forcing Outliers to strip. There was no way she could get away with it. Not for long. Even if the Sovereign had no idea who had taken the baby, they would know it was an Outlier. The mother of this baby, whoever she was, would send the Fortis here to wipe us out. Not just us, but every Outlier village in the wilds.

"She has to take it back," I said, raising my voice so it could be heard over my pounding heart, which was thudding so loudly I was unable to focus on anything else.

Adina put her hand on my arm and gave me a smile that was supposed to be reassuring, but all it managed to do was frighten me even more. Why was she unconcerned? Like all the Outliers without jobs in the city, she avoided going close to the walls, avoided the Fortis, but she had to understand how dangerous this situation could be. Everyone did.

"Be calm, Indra. The child was not stolen. It was given to her."

Bodhi spoke before I could recover from my shock. "What do you mean?"

Adina began walking, nodding for us to follow. "The Sovereign are very strict about their laws, and not just with Outliers. Population control is one of their main goals since they have no more room to expand inside the city, and when they decreed that every other generation must have only one child, they meant it."

"Someone broke the law and had another baby?" I asked in disbelief.

Adina shrugged as if the Sovereign breaking their own rules was nothing new. "It happens more than you would think. The law says that these babies are to be turned out, or left to die after they are born. But not everyone obeys the law, and those who do not wish to see their child die turn to us."

"They just hand their babies over to the Outliers?" Bodhi asked, shaking his head. "They hate us."

Adina shrugged again, but I was barely paying attention when she responded to him. I was too busy thinking about something that he had not picked up on. Something that he probably would not have even considered since he had never set foot inside the city and had no idea just how difficult it was to get in and out unnoticed.

"How did Xandra get the baby out of the city without being seen?" I asked, cutting Adina off mid-sentence. "She could not have gone through the gate. They would have seen her."

Adina finally stopped walking and turned to face us.

"There is an underground tunnel that leads in and out of the city. It is well hidden and its location is known only by a select few, both inside and outside the walls, but it exists for circumstances such as these."

"There is another way into the city?" Bodhi's voice was higher than usual, and his blue eyes bright. As if this news was a gift that had been given to him. "A back way?"

Adina nodded slowly, but her narrowed eyes told me that she was as concerned by his interest as I was. "It is nothing you should ever consider, Bodhi. If the Sovereign are willing to kill their own babies, what do you think they would do to an intruder? Especially an Outlier."

"I was not thinking of going there myself," Bodhi said, but his tone was neither convincing nor comforting.

Adina's gaze moved to me, and I could see the warning in it. Like Bodhi, she had never set foot inside the city — at least that I knew of — but she was well aware of what happened inside the walls because she was our village healer. I had gone to her after Lysander cornered me in the pantry, and I was not alone in that. I knew what she was warning me about, knew that she was telling me to be careful what I told Bodhi, but her concern was unnecessary. Even before this conversation, I told my husband very little about the city, and now I was more certain than ever that I had been right to keep things from him. It was no longer just about keeping him from sharing my pain. It was about keeping him alive.

THIRTEEN

ODHI WAS QUIET AFTER WE LEFT THE VILLAGE. He walked a step ahead of me, his right hand clutching mine, and a torch in his other. The light from the fire flickered off the naked branches above our heads and highlighted the ruins from the old world that occasionally jutted up, poking their skeletal remains through the long dead leaves and snow packed on the ground. The remnants of that world were nothing more than rusted shells and stone lumps that were impossible to identify. There was very little left of the past in the wilds, and even less in the wastelands, but what did exist was a total mystery to me. To all of us, probably.

Everything we knew about the people who had once lived on this land had been passed down through word of mouth over the years. In Sovereign City they had books, their pages containing lines and lines of symbols I could not decipher and would most likely be unable to comprehend even if I could, but I had no way of knowing if the stories in those books were the same ones I had grown up hearing.

The Outliers spoke of a world that had at one time been overcrowded, yet fertile. The people of the past had lived close together like the Sovereign, packed into cities and numbering more than the stars in the sky. Electricity was everywhere, and the technology the Sovereign possessed paled in comparison to what it had been back then. These things had made life easier, but legend told us that it had also led to the destruction of their world.

They had fought with one another, all these cities that were now buried under dust. What they had fought over none of us knew for certain, but we did know that it had not only destroyed them, but had also left the earth barren and dry. Their wars had changed the ground we now stood on, poisoning it for future generations. Decades went by before the land had healed enough to allow the wilds to sprout up, but by then the Sovereign had already built their city in the wastelands. The people outside the walls, the ones who had been left to fend for themselves, had split into groups and done what they could to survive. Some had remained close to the city, depending on the generosity of those inside to keep them alive, while others had struck out and settled in the wilds. The greenery had given them hope that things would get better, but still the land had not healed itself completely, and so they waited.

Time passed and very little changed. The wastelands were still more immense than any other part of our world, stretching on as far as the eye could see in most directions.

The land the Outliers lived on was green, but the soil still yielded poor crops. The Sovereign still hid behind their walls while the rest of us served them. This had been the order of things for centuries, and would no doubt remain the same for centuries to come.

By the time Bodhi and I reached a rocky part of the forest, the sky was nearly black. Here the rocks jutted up and widened into a stony mass that was not tall enough to be called a mountain, but was much too big to simply be a hill. It was here that Bodhi stopped and turned to face me for the first time since leaving the village.

"This is it."

When he smiled it seemed to take a lot of effort, and I hated how hard he had to work to appear happy. Hated that what Adina had told us sat so heavy on him. Not just because it hurt me to see him in pain, but also because it was proof that he knew more about what went on inside the city than I suspected. Bodhi was good at hiding it, but he had done so because there was nothing he could do to change the way things were. Now that he knew there was another way into the city, it seemed like he was reflecting on everything more. Like he might be considering what he could do to even the score.

"You brought me to a giant rock?" I asked with a smile of my own, hoping to bring back the easy grin I was used to seeing on my husband's face.

Some of the lightheartedness returned to his expression when he said, "No. I brought you to my secret hideout."

I looked from him to the rock at our side, but saw nothing that looked like a hideout.

As a child I had gone out into the woods with Bodhi often, but years had passed since I had ventured into the forest, and even back then we had never wandered far. The Outliers were not like the Sovereign. The women were not rulers, and we did not see ourselves as indestructible. Inside the city Saffron could bark an order and it would be carried out in the blink of an eye, but in the wild world beyond those walls, the Fortis would never bow to a woman's command. It was much too common for Outlier women to be attacked if they ventured too far from their villages. Bodhi had been around to protect me when I was younger, but I had seen women brought in, dead or wishing they were, and I had always been too afraid to go very far. Even with him.

Before I could ask what he had meant about a hideout, Bodhi took my hand and pulled me closer to the rocky hill at his side. When we were next to it he released my hand and held the torch out for me to take. Then he moved a mass of vines and branches aside, revealing a hole in the rocks.

"A cave?"

I ducked lower so I could get a look inside. The hole was small, wide enough that we would be able to pass through but so low that we would need to duck to get in. Thanks to the light from the torch, I could tell that it went deep and opened up inside.

"Yes," Bodhi replied from behind me. "And tomorrow I will teach you how to shoot a bow."

When I glanced back at him, I had no doubt that my eyes were shimmering with surprise. "Winta women do not hunt."

"I want you to be prepared in case something happens to

me."

I stood up straight and turned to face my husband, the cave in front of me forgotten. "What are you saying?"

He did not blink when he said, "Just that life in the wilds is hard and things happen. It is unfair that women are left to fend for themselves but given no skills to do it."

"The village helps them," I argued even though I agreed with him.

When my father died, we were forced to accept the leftover meat from other families in the village. Families who still had a man to go out into the woods to hunt. I remember eating the meat of a forest cat, tough with fat, and wishing I was allowed to venture into the woods to find food the way the men in the village were. At the same time, however, I never would have done it even if I had been allowed. I was a woman, which meant that I was too weak and small to protect myself from the animals, let alone a Fortis hunter if I happened upon one.

"I believe women are capable of helping themselves and I want to make sure you are able to." Bodhi took the torch from my hand and nodded to the cave. "Now, follow me."

He moved forward, keeping both the flame and his head low as he ducked through the hole in front of us. He shuffled through at a crouch that looked both practiced and proficient while I crawled in behind him on my hands and knees. Once we were inside, the room opened up so that the ceiling towered over our heads, making it possible for me to stand. It was bigger than any of the huts in our village, and the openings at the back told me this was only one of many rooms.

"What do you think?" Bodhi asked as he moved forward.

"Amazing," I said in awe.

He knelt in front of a pile of wood, and I watched as he used the torch to start a fire, which took no time at all.

"Will it fill the cave with smoke?"

Bodhi grinned up at me from where he knelt by the now crackling fire. "There are a few holes in the rocks here, see." He pointed to the sloped ceiling over his head. "I have to make sure they do not get clogged when the leaves fall off the trees in the fall, but as long as I keep the holes free of debris they do a good job of venting the smoke."

Once he was certain that the fire would not go out, he crossed the cave yet again. On the other side he had mounds of animal fur stored in a crevice, and more wood piled up so he could keep the fire going.

Bodhi spread the fur out near, but not too close, to the fire and then settled back. When he patted the fur at his side, I went over to join him on the ground, snuggling up next to him.

"Why have you never brought me here before?"

"I wanted to wait until we were married. That way it could be our special place."

I looked up from where my head was resting against his chest, peering at him through my eyelashes, and found his blue eyes trained on me.

"You were always sure I would eventually marry you?" I whispered.

He pressed his lips against my forehead, right over the passage markings that still throbbed slightly. "I never had a doubt."

I laughed and scooted closer so he could wrap me in his warm embrace. We sat in silence, staring at the fire. Enjoying this quiet moment together. Before long my thoughts were once again on the things Adina had told us. Talking about it felt like fanning the flames of whatever thoughts Bodhi had swirling through his head, but I was afraid that not discussing it would only give those ideas time to stew.

Finally, I broke the silence by whispering, "I want you to promise that you will never try to sneak into the city. No matter what happens."

"Indra," he began.

I cut him off by sitting up so I could look him in the eye, and what I saw there terrified me. So much pain. More than I had ever seen before. Where had it come from? What had happened to cause him to hurt this much?

"I am serious, Bodhi." He started to look away, but I took his face between my hands and forced his eyes to stay on mine. "If they catch you, they will kill you. Do you understand that? Do you understand what that would do to me?"

"What about me?" he whispered. "You have no idea what it does to me, knowing all the things you have been through, but being unable to do anything about it."

Tears filled my eyes at the knowledge that he was hurting, but the pain I knew I would feel if something were to happen to him overshadowed it. "And you think dying would be doing something?"

Bodhi tried to turn his head again, but I refused to let him. Instead, he squeezed his eyes shut and let out a deep breath. "I might not die."

"Bodhi—"

His name came out as a strangled gasp, and even if I could have managed to utter another word, there would have been no time before he said, "I was there, Indra, I saw you."

My heartbeat thudded against my temples, making it impossible to understand what he was talking about. "What do you mean?"

"Three years ago, right after you started working in the city, I was waiting for you to get back from work. I was at the front of the village at first, but then Anja asked me to help her carry some wood to your hut. I was on my way back when I saw you outside Adina's hut. You were shaking. Even from a distance I could tell. I know you so well—know all your emotions and reactions—and I knew right away that something bad had happened. I was about to call out to you when Adina opened her door, and when you saw her, you started crying."

Bodhi finally managed to turn his face away, but my hands did not drop to my sides. They stayed suspended in the air as if I had forgotten how to use my arms. I had never heard this. Had not known that he had been present to witness my shame, and I hated it.

He was still looking away when he started talking again. "I have known all this time what happened, but I could never talk to you about it because I knew you would never want me to. It has almost killed me at times, thinking about what you went through. Thinking about—"

His voice broke, and when he squeezed his eyes shut, a tear rolled down his cheek. Years had passed since the last time I saw Bodhi cry. We had been young then, only seven years old, and he had fallen out of a tree and broken his arm. Seeing the tears in his eyes now nearly broke *me* the same way his arm had broken that day.

"Bodhi," I whispered. I found myself moving closer, putting my arms around him. "Do not cry." I kissed his cheek, and when his shoulders shook, my own tears spilled over. "There is nothing you could have done and I am okay. I promise."

He cried harder, wrapping his arms around me and holding on like I was the only thing keeping him from floating away.

This was the very thing I had been trying to avoid, Bodhi taking on *my* pain. I had no desire to see him hurting because of what I had gone through, had no desire for him to think that he was somehow responsible for saving me when there was nothing that could be done. It was too much responsibility, and I knew that if he took it on, the weight of it would eventually kill him.

"Promise me," I said between sobs. "Promise me that you will never try to go into the city. *Promise.*"

He nodded, possibly too choked up to get any words out, and I foolishly took it as agreement.

FOURTEEN

A S AN OUTLIER WORKING IN THE CITY, I GOT ONE day off every two weeks, and for my first one as Bodhi's wife, I chose to spend the entire day with him. We slept in the cave, curled up on top of a pile of furs. Between the fire going at our side and the warmth of my husband's body, there was no chance for a chill to sink into my bones, and even the hard floor of the cave was unable to keep me from snagging a good night's sleep.

The scurry of feet in the dark recesses of the cave woke me in the morning. Sunshine streamed in through the holes Bodhi had pointed out the night before, and I had to turn my eyes away from the light. They were small, placed at a level that was both good for venting the smoke from the fire, but also would not allow too much water in if we had a rare night of rain.

I had only been awake for a moment when Bodhi turned to face me. His eyes were hazy with sleep and puffy from the night before, but the smile that lit up his face was closer to the expression I was used to seeing.

"Sleep well?" he asked.

"Every night that I am with you, I will sleep well."

I snuggled against him and the sigh he let out seemed to sink into me.

"Good," he said.

He kissed the top of my head before untangling himself and climbing to his feet. I was naked, so I pulled the fur up to my chin and watched as he built the fire back up. Bodhi was still undressed as well, and I expected him to worry about sparks, but he seemed unconcerned.

"Hungry?" he called over his shoulder, his focus on the fire in front of him.

"Of course."

He looked back, shooting me a grin that lit up his face, and then pulled a leather pouch from his bag and tossed it my way. It was filled with dried fruit and meat, as well as a handful of nuts. Not much, especially for two people, but this was the way we lived and something we were both used to after a lifetime of struggle.

He came back and sat at my side, and together we ate, naked but warmed by the fire.

"What is beyond this room?" I asked, nodding to the other tunnels. "Have you explored more of the cave?"

"Some," he replied, "but not much. A larger room sits just beyond the tunnel, but there is no light and no holes for ventilation. Further back are even more tunnels. I explored them once, but they seemed to go on forever and I realized that if my torch burned out I could get lost and die. It seemed too risky."

I shivered and scooted closer. "Yes, it does."

After we finished eating, we staunched out the fire and left the cave. Bodhi had his bow, as well as a smaller one for me, and even though his offer the night before had surprised me, I was looking forward to learning how to shoot. It was something I had done a handful of times when we were kids, but I had been forced to give up after my father's death. At the time my mother worked in the city, and the responsibility of looking after Anja had fallen completely on my shoulders.

"Do you always hunt this far from the village?" I asked Bodhi as we moved away from the cave.

"Not always." When he looked at me, his dimples were showing. "I like to stay close so I can be back by the time you get home."

I squeezed his hand, remembering all the days over the years when he seemed to pop up the moment I returned from Sovereign City.

"Why are we out so far today?"

"I wanted to show you something. Remember?"

"I thought the cave was what you wanted to show me."

"It was part of what I wanted to show you, but not all of it." Bodhi pulled on my hand and walked faster up the slope of the hill in front of us. "Come on."

The hill got steeper, rockier too, and more difficult to climb, but Bodhi clung to my hand as he went and it helped keep me on my feet. We seemed to walk forever, and I was just about to ask him once again where we were going when we reached the top and he stopped. I did as well, but the awe I felt at the sight made it impossible to speak at first.

Only a few feet in front of us, the hill we had worked so hard to climb ended in a cliff. It was impossible to tell how far down the drop was, but it was far enough that a fall from here would no doubt end in death. The cliff was not what made me freeze, although that was a sight to behold, it was what loomed in the distance. A city. Or the ruins of one, anyway.

It must have been a huge city, because even now it seemed to go on so far that I was unable to discern where it ended. The ruins of a few tall buildings jutted up here and there, most of them so in shambles that even from a distance they seemed ready to crumble, but the majority of the buildings looked as if they had been leveled hundreds of years ago, and what remained were only outlines of what had once been there.

"Is this real?" I gasped.

"It is. Pretty amazing, right?"

I nodded, only amazing seemed like the wrong word. It was common knowledge that a different world had existed centuries ago and that something—no one knew for sure what—had wiped it out, but before now I had never seen more than a handful of the ruins. Where we lived very little was left of the old world, and what remained was usually unrecognizable. Here I could easily imagine where the buildings had stood, could picture them towering over the ground as clearly as if they were in front of me now. Time and nature had not been kind to the city, but it was still possible to make out where the roads had been, and where the vehicles from that old world had once traveled.

"It would be nice to go there one day," Bodhi said. "Not just there, but beyond it. Sometimes, I find myself sitting here for hours thinking about it. Wondering what might be out there and if it is better than the life we have here."

"There has to be something better," I whispered.

Bodhi squeezed my hand and turned to face me. "We could go. You know that, right? It would be hard, but if we were together we could make it."

"What?"

Bodhi had never talked like this before, and I was uncertain how to respond. Could he be serious? No one ever left the area, there were too many unknown dangers out there, things that might make lygan and grizzards seem like cuddly babies. But when I searched my husband's face, I realized that Bodhi was completely serious. What was more, he had brought me here for this very reason.

I dropped his hand and stepped back. "Bodhi, you know I cannot."

"Think about it." He grabbed me by the shoulders as if he was trying to get my attention even though he already had it. "If we left you would never have to worry about the Sovereign or the Fortis again. We could go somewhere new. Start a life in a new place, maybe with new people. We could get away from here."

"I can't leave my mother and Anja, Bodhi. You have to know that."

"They can come with us."

It hurt to see the excitement and hope in his eyes. I hated to be the one who took that from him, but I had to. What he was suggesting was crazy and unrealistic, and much too risky.

"My mother is sick," I said gently. "She would never make it, and Anja would never leave her behind, even if I would. Which was impossible. We have no way of knowing if there is even anything out there. Think about that, Bodhi." I pulled from his grasp and turned to face the ruins, and he did as well. "Getting there would take hours of traveling through the wastelands, and that would only be the beginning. Living in the ruins would be impossible. We would be worse off than we are in the wilds, so we would have to walk more. Who knows how long it would take to reach something beyond that or if it would even be better? Odds are that there is nothing better than the wilds. That there is nothing but wastelands."

When I turned back to face him, Bodhi's smile had melted away, and I felt the loss of it. Felt as if I had reached out and stolen his happiness.

"I know." He let out a deep sigh, followed only a second later by a bitter laugh. "It was a silly dream, but it was nice."

I stepped closer, slipping my hand into his and resting my head on his shoulder. "It would be nice to go away, but you know we will be okay here. As long as we are together, we can make it."

He kissed the top of my head and whispered, "I know." Something in his tone made me shiver.

WE LEFT THE DREAMS OF LIFE BEYOND THE WILDS behind and climbed back down the hill. After our conversation, I was afraid Bodhi would be too dejected to teach me to shoot. Thankfully he recovered quickly.

We practiced first, me shooting the bow a few times while he gave me pointers. More than ten years had passed since I had held one of the weapons in my hands. Back then I had been a good shot, and a few tries told me that time had not taken that skill from me. Bodhi was all praise, telling me that I was a natural. It boosted my confidence even more as I fired arrow after arrow at the tree.

When I had perfected hitting a wide trunk, we moved on to a smaller one, and then an even smaller one until I finally missed. When that happened I tried again, missing the tree three more times before finally hitting it. Each time I released an arrow my aim seemed to improve, much to Bodhi's delight, and before long he declared that I was ready to go hunting.

The snow made it easy to track animals through the forest, and Bodhi took his time showing me how to tell the difference between new tracks and old ones, as well as the best places to find big game. Forest cats were unpredictable he told me, but much easier to find and kill during winter than rodents were. He was right, and after following a set of tracks for nearly an hour, we came upon a cat that was right in the middle of eating one of the very rodents that had managed to evade us.

A variety of cats lived in the wilds, some with long brown hair that seemed more fitting for blending into the wastelands than the greenery of the forest, while others had pelts decorated with stripes or spots. The one in front of us now had a swirl of gray and black fur; its stripes intermixed with spots. It was smaller than Bodhi, but bigger than me, and had teeth as pointed as the tip of an arrowhead.

"Perfect," Bodhi whispered when he saw that the cat was distracted. "Now is your chance."

I raised my bow and took aim, going through the same motions I had while practicing on the trees. The cat was mostly still, only its head moving as it tore into its dinner, and I knew I could take it out. All I had to do was release the arrow and I would have my very first kill.

A branch snapped to our left and the cat's head jerked up. Bodhi grabbed my arm and pulled me down so fast I almost released my arrow anyway. We were behind a bush, and for a moment I thought we were hiding from the cat, but then I saw how big Bodhi's eyes were, and I knew it was something else. A lygan, maybe? They rarely ventured into the wilds, but it did happen from time to time. Only, if that were the case it would have charged already. Even at twice its size, a forest cat would be no match for a lygan.

A spear sailed from the trees to our right a beat after the thought entered my head and I nearly let out a yelp of surprise. As if sensing it, Bodhi's hand covered my mouth. His palms were clammy despite the cool day, and he was as still as the now dead animal in front of us, and it was not until a moment before the Fortis man stepped into view that I realized exactly *what* we were hiding from.

He was big, just like they all were, and the dark clothes he wore stood out against the snowy ground. His red hair was wild and his blue eyes piercing as they narrowed on the cat. It was as if he thought the animal might only be playing dead. When the cat made no move, the man yanked the spear from its body and slipped it into a holster on his back. Blood dripped from the point and landed on the snow, starkly red against the white blanket on the forest floor.

My legs ached from crouching, but I remained frozen in place. We could see everything from where we were, and I was terrified that if this man looked our way he would spot us immediately. And so I held my breath and remained still. At my side Bodhi did the same, while in the clearing the man hefted the cat's body up off the ground with a grunt. Then he turned, his gaze moving over the trees where we hid but not focusing on anything for longer than a beat. When he let out a whistle, the clump of footsteps was followed by the appearance of a horse pushing its way through the trees and into the clearing.

Bodhi and I remained hidden and still as the man loaded his kill onto the animal, and it was at that moment that a strange thought entered my head. We could kill him. Hidden the way we were, he would never see it coming. I could lift my bow and take aim and kill this man before he even realized we were there, and his death would mean one less Fortis was around to torture my people.

As quickly as the thought entered my mind, I pushed it away. Killing a person, even someone so unworthy of life, was wrong. It was not up to me, a simple Outlier, to decide who got to live and who got to die. Let God rain his judgment down on the Fortis in His own time.

When the man had finally climbed onto his horse and ridden away, Bodhi let out a sigh of relief and pulled his hand from my mouth. "That was close."

My heart was still pounding wildly, echoing in my ears and nearly drowning out my words when I asked, "Do you see them often?"

"No. They usually stick to the valley, close to the river. In winter it can be hard to find game though, and they end up coming deeper into the wilds." He stood, pulling me with him. "You just need to keep your ears open out here."

"I will," I whispered.

I was thinking about this man, about what would have happened if he had snuck up on us, but also about how my husband would have reacted if I had killed him. Would Bodhi have been disgusted? Would he have looked at me with the same pride and admiration as he had after I killed the lygan? I had no way of knowing.

At my side, Bodhi frowned and looked around. "Now we need to find a new set of tracks."

He had been right to say that game was harder to come by in winter, and it took us several hours of exploring the snowy forest before we were able to locate another animal. It was a cat once again, this one with fur that was nearly as white as the blanket of snow covering the wilds. Just like before, I took aim, only this time no Fortis guard showed up to ruin the shot. My arrow flew through the air before finding a home in the animal. The cat let out a roar and reared back before taking off, and Bodhi and I were right behind him. He only made it a short distance before succumbing to his wounds though, and by the time we came upon him, he had already taken his last breath.

Bodhi smiled at me before pulling the arrow from the cat's body. "It is a good kill."

I returned his smile as I took the arrow and replaced it in my quiver, but I said nothing. This was not the first animal I had killed, but it was the first I had tracked and hunted, and the knowledge filled me with something impossible to name. It made me stand taller.

Bodhi dropped to his knees beside the animal and I followed his lead, taking a knee beside him. When my husband bowed his head, his blond hair fell over his forehead, covering his passage markings.

His eyes were shut, but I kept my gaze on him as he began to recite the simple prayer our people reserved for the passing of animals, the words low and reverent. "May your death provide life to our people and sustain us through hard times."

He was only halfway through the prayer when my gaze moved to the cat, and this time I recognized the rush of pride that swept through me. This was my kill, and the meat of this animal would help feed not just my family, but also others in the village. For the first time I felt like I was able to provide so much more than just what the Sovereign gave me, and it made me feel useful, strong even. It was a feeling I was unused to, but one I liked.

FIFTEEN

IFE IN THE CITY GREW MORE AND MORE complicated as time passed, but back in my village, in my role of Bodhi's wife, things were serene. We continued to hunt, me improving every day, and went to the cave often to get away from life in the village. My mother was stronger than she had been, something I attributed to the extra protein she was now getting, and I began to hope that her condition would improve instead of grow worse. That she might live long enough to see grandchildren, not just from Bodhi and myself, but from Anja as well.

Spring bloomed early in the wilds and the heat of the wastelands became more intense. The animals living both there and on the cliffs grew more active, making our trek to and from work more difficult. My aim with the bow improved each time Bodhi took me into the forest, and before long I began to carry my bow instead of just a knife, knowing that it would give Mira and me an advantage if we had another confrontation with a lygan.

My aim was not the only thing that had grown, Bodhi's confidence in me had as well. With that confidence, my uneasiness about why he was teaching me to shoot also grew. His explanation that he wanted me to be able to take care of myself rang true, but with it came the knowledge that he had thought, more than once, about me being alone. Did that mean he was also thinking about coming into the city to avenge me? The more I thought about it, the more I worried that he might do something rash, and every night when I settled into bed at my husband's side, I prayed that nothing would happen to force his hand.

It was shortly after every spot of snow had melted from the wilds that the next big change sprang up. Mira and I had both been off work the day before—she had spent time resting while Bodhi and I had once again gone to our cave—and during our absence something had happened in the Fortis village. We spotted it from a distance as we stopped just past the Lygan Cliffs to stash our weapons; only it was hard to tell exactly what was going on.

"What do you think it is?" Mira asked.

I shook my head, unable to come up with even a guess. In three years of working in Sovereign City, I had never seen the Fortis do much—at least not in their village. Now though, they were visible in the distance moving planks of wood, and the bang of what could only be hammers echoed through the air.

"Building something," I said. "What, I have no clue."

"Asa would know," Mira replied.

I glanced her way, knowing that it was not intended as a jab but feeling the sting of it anyway. No matter what I did, it was impossible to completely push away my guilt over the situation. There was nothing going on between Asa and me, but I knew he had feelings for me and that he was putting himself at risk on a daily basis because of those feelings. It had not been at my request, as Mira had pointed out at least a dozen times, but it still felt wrong.

Then there was Bodhi. My husband, who I loved. He was all I wanted, but at times the secrets between us felt as insurmountable as the wilds that spread out beyond the ruins we had stood on the hill and looked down on. Even though the secrets were for his protection, I still hated that it had to be this way. I knew Asa was genuine in his desire to help me and that there with no strings attached, but Bodhi's only experience with the Fortis were the times they had attacked innocent women from our tribe or killed our hunters when they were in the forest. He would never trust Asa, and I was terrified of what he might do if he found out what was going on. Of the promises he might break.

Mira and I moved through the Fortis village, heading to the gate, but still we were given no hints as to what was being built. The streets were typically deserted this early in the morning, and today was no exception, and we made it to the wall with no interference.

When the gate opened in front of us, we trudged inside. It scared me how foreign the streets now felt. Where once the walk to and from Saffron's house had been relaxing, it now felt as if we were running a gauntlet of danger. Every guard who looked our way seemed to have a sneer on his face, every dark corner felt as if it held doom. We practically ran now, and I would be lying if I said I did not look for Asa's face everywhere we went. He alone would be able to save us if one of the men we passed decided to take advantage of his position, which was yet another thing I had to feel guilty about. Bodhi was supposed to be the one who protected me. Not Asa.

We were out of breath by the time we made it to the house, but thankfully we were also unharmed. Mira and I stormed in, gasping, and nearly tripped over a Fortis man who for some reason was standing in the middle of the mudroom. My heart skipped once before I saw who it was, but in a blink the terror was gone and had been replaced by relief.

"Asa," I said, gasping out his name.

Heat flooded to my cheeks and I had to look away when memories of the night before came rushing back. Bodhi on top of me and of how I had gasped out his name in much the same way as I had Asa's just now.

The Fortis guard gave his usual silent greeting, a nod that seemed to say twice as much as most people said with words, and Mira mimicked him, her eyes down the way they always were when in his presence. She trusted him now, of that I was sure, but she was unused to looking anyone in the eye within the walls of this city, and I doubted she would ever get over that. After everything, it was a shock that I managed to pull it off.

She grabbed her apron and hurried off, shooting me a look that said she wanted me to ask about what they were building in the Fortis village. I knew I would, as much for me as for her, but the idea of being alone with Asa made me nervous.

I waited until she was gone before turning to him, and what came out of my mouth had nothing to do with the building in his village. "You were waiting for me?"

His head bobbed again, just once, and his eyes stayed on me, focused and intense enough to make my scalp prickle. "I wanted to make sure you were okay. I didn't see you yesterday."

"It was my day off," I said, doing my best to act as if his gaze did not make my skin tingle.

"I know."

His words made me blush yet again, and I had to look away. He had known it was my day off, which meant that his motivation behind waiting for me had not been concern for my well being. He had missed me.

"My husband and I went hunting." Bodhi was already present in the room, I could feel him hanging between us, but I still flushed again at the mention of him.

"Did you get anything?"

"A forest cat," I replied, my eyes still down.

Asa said nothing, and I looked up through my lashes to find him watching me the way he always did, with emotion in his brown eyes that had no business being there.

I took a step back. "What are they building in your village?"

"You saw that." It was his turn to look away, and when he did he let out a deep breath that sounded almost painful.

"I did."

"It's something new the Sovereign have come up with. I don't know all the details, but I've heard they will be quarters. For Outliers."

I blinked as if the action would help me understand what he was telling me, but everything remained as jumbled as it had before. "What? Who?"

Asa hesitated before saying, "For the people who work in the city."

It took me a moment to register this, but when I did I had no clue how to respond. They were building quarters. For Outliers. In the Fortis village. My mind went wild, wondering if we would have a choice in the matter and if they planned on locking us inside at night. I found myself torn between the hope that we would be locked in, and the hope that we would not. If the doors were locked it would mean we were prisoners, which I had no doubt was Paizlee's plan. She did not want servants, she wanted slaves, and this got her one step closer. But if the doors were kept unlocked, it would be easier for the Fortis to get inside whenever they wanted. It would be easier for them to take whoever they wanted in whatever manner they wished.

Then a much more terrifying possibility occurred to me. Who would be allowed to live in this building? There was no way it would be large enough for entire families, meaning they expected us to leave our family behind. Our parents, siblings, husbands, and wives. The thought of living without Bodhi was inconceivable. This might mean choosing between him and my job, an impossible decision, but no job meant my family would struggle.

"Are you okay?"

My head jerked up at the sound of Asa's voice. I had become so lost in my own thoughts that I had completely forgotten he was standing in front of me.

"No," I mumbled as I shook my head. "I need to talk to Saffron."

I passed Asa and headed into the kitchen. Mira was there, already preparing lunch, and she shot me a worried look that I ignored. I should have been heading upstairs to strip the beds so I could wash the sheets, but I was unable to. Not until I knew what was going to happen.

Saffron's office was empty, and so I headed to her study. There I found her drinking a glass of wine and reading. It was still early morning, but it was a normal sight to see her with a drink at this time of day. When someone had no work to do, there was no reason not to indulge.

"Mistress," I said, stopping in the doorway so I could curtsy. I left my head down, waiting for her to respond.

"Yes." She snapped her book shut much harder than necessary. "What is it, Indra?"

"I wanted to ask you a question if you are free."

Saffron let out a long sigh, but I glanced up to find her gray eyes shimmering with curiosity. "Go on, then."

"I have heard that they are building quarters in the Fortis village and that the Outliers working in the city will be expected to live there. Is this true?"

This time when she exhaled, she also got to her feet. "It is. Stateswoman Paizlee proposed the bill last year but it failed. I'm afraid that the stunt your little friend pulled was enough to scare people, and this time when she put it through, it passed. By a *landslide*."

She over pronounced the last word, but it was not her tone that made me feel as if a pile of dirt were falling down on my head. It was the next question that popped into my head.

"What about families?" I whispered.

Saffron frowned. "Speak up, Indra."

"What about my family?" I said louder.

"You can't expect us to make room for *all* of you." I opened my mouth to speak, but Saffron cut me off by saying, "This will be a good thing, Indra. Mark my words. I'll admit I had reservations about it, but Paizlee is right. If we give you what you *need* there will be no need to steal. This will mean you have food and a roof over head when it rains or snows. It will mean you won't have to walk so far to work."

"But I have a husband," I said. "I am married now."

Saffron shook her head, and despite the sympathetic smile she gave me, there was no emotion in her gray eyes. "It's new. You'll get over him and find someone else. Someone who also works in the city." Her eyes rolled a little but I could tell she was trying to stop them. "Trust me. Men are more trouble than they're worth."

She must have considered the matter closed, because she turned her back on me and picked up her glass. "Now go to work before I have to reduce your rations."

I did as I was told, but my mind was only half on my work. All I could think about was the choice I would soon face: leave my job or leave Bodhi. Leaving my husband was impossible, and losing my position meant having the job that had been in our family for generations ripped away from us for good, as well as losing the medicine my mother depended on. My decision would affect everyone in my family, and everyone who would one day be in my family. It would affect Anja and my mother. It would mean that I would have to find some other way to pitch in so we did not starve.

Maybe Bodhi had been right.

The thought hit me halfway through the day, right in the middle of remaking the beds I had already stripped. I thought back to the first day he had taken me to the cave, how he had suggested we leave. I had scoffed at him then, but if there was nothing keeping me here, if I was going to lose the only real security we had, why should I stay? My mother was the only real reason I could come up with, and even though she was a big one, I told myself there had to be a way to make it work. It would be impossible for her to walk far, but if we had a cart or something we could pull her. Maybe.

I thought about the cliff Bodhi and I had stood on, looking down over the city ruins. About the debris from hundreds of years ago that was no doubt littering the streets. Would there be a way to survive out there? Was there anything beyond it? Another city? Perhaps one that stood in a green area much like the wilds. It was impossible to know for sure, but I knew I had to figure something out by the time that building was finished. However long that took.

HOUSEMAID WAS A COVETED POSITION INSIDE THE walls, and one my family had held for generations. Only the most trusted people were given the positions since it required close contact with the family and their belongings, but for Outliers it had more to do with *where* it kept you. Inside. In the artificially cool air when the heat from the summer sun pounded down on the city, away from the dangers of the streets and the threat of getting caught outside during a grizzard attack. It was an extra safety cushion in an uncertain world.

It was a position I had enjoyed, as much as I could enjoy anything in the city, but since Ronan's punishment, Saffron had taken to sending me on random errands throughout the city. Something she had rarely done before. The new post would not have bothered me quite as much before—the threats outside were all very real and dangerous, but the dangers inside the house were just as real. Now though, with everything in the city that had changed, being out in the open was unwelcome. Especially on my own.

Warmer weather had arrived, and even though the wilds had not yet reached the scorching temperatures of summer, and the same could probably be said of the Fortis village, it took very little for Sovereign City to heat up. The high walls, the houses packed in tightly, and the narrow streets all worked together to trap in the sun's heat. I knew from experience that it would get much worse when spring moved into summer, but the streets were already stifling when I left Saffron's house after lunch. The roads were crowded with Outliers who, like me, were running errands for the Sovereign house they worked in, but there were also plenty of Fortis guards around. An occasional Sovereign could even been seen in the crowd, always with a guard just in case and always covered by a robe to protect their pale skin from the dangers of the sun, and the people were packed in so tightly that by the time I reached the end of the street my dress was sticking to my back.

In the distance I heard the crack of a whip, as well as the cry of agony that followed it, and the sounds bounced off the walls around me as I moved. A Fortis guard bumped me as I walked faster, hoping to escape the sounds, and I found myself shoved to the side as he grumbled under his breath about clumsy Outliers. Through the crowd I caught sight of two Fortis women laughing at a man. He was from the Mountari tribe, and his shirt had been removed to reveal dozens of lygan teeth decorating his arms and chest. Why he had been forced to strip I was unable to say, but just before I looked away, one of the Fortis women yanked a tooth from his flesh.

I walked faster, keeping my head down in the hope that it would protect me from having to witness anything else.

My first stop was the bakery, which was a relief not just because I wanted to escape the sights and sounds on the street, but also because the building was cool thanks to the artificial air. A small crowd was already waiting to get bread when I stepped through the door. It only took one scan of the group to see that no one from my tribe was present. A Huni woman caught my gaze for the briefest of moments before she looked away. Sweat glistened on her shaved head, which was a blistering pink from the sun. What appeared to be several teeth from a lygan pierced the top of her right ear, and the talon of a rawlin was stuck through the lobe of the other. The brief glimpse I had gotten of her face showed other piercings, through her nose and eyebrows and even her lip. The Huni, like the Mountari, associated with other tribes as little as possible, but I knew enough about them to know that each of the woman's piercings represented a moment in her life in much the same way that my passage markings commemorated mine. Still, the thought of having a lygan tooth shoved through my skin sent a shudder shooting through me. I much preferred our passage markings.

Even though the Trelite woman at her side was more welcoming, her only greeting for me was still a simple nod. Our two tribes were at least on good terms even if we rarely intermixed. The Huni avoided everyone other than their own people as much as possible, and the Mountari were not much better. It was a waste in my opinion. The Outliers outnumbered the Sovereign and Fortis put together, but *together* was something we had never considered.

Behind the counter another Huni woman took orders from the Outliers crowded into the store. In the back, one of her coworkers was busy baking more bread, which would be sold by the woman behind the counter to other Outliers. Except all of it was for the Sovereign. The bread was baked by Outlier hands and sold to other Outliers, but all the money exchanged and all the bread bought went to the Sovereign. They collected the money and they ate the food we prepared, and yet we did all the work. This was the way it had always been, and unless something changed it would always be this way.

When it was my turn I found that Saffron's order was ready and waiting for me—two loaves that were still warm—and I took them gratefully before returning to the street. The heat of their crusty goodness only added to my discomfort and I was anxious to get home, but the crowd was just as thick as it had been on my walk to the bakery and I had two more stops to make. The butcher to get a roast for dinner, and the tailor to pick up the dress Saffron was to wear for Lysander's wedding.

The screams were the first sign that something was wrong. They started deep in the city, a street or more away from me, and were so muffled that at first I wondered if I had heard them at all. Then the sound rippled through the crowd, making people around me slow or stop and even a few run faster. That was when it hit me what was happening.

The first grizzard came out of nowhere, screeching through the air as it swooped down the street only a foot above the crowd. The bird was colossal, with a wingspan that barely gave it room to fly between the buildings and a long neck that allowed it to scan the street below as it flew. Its black feathers were iridescent in the light of the sun, reflecting blues and greens and purples, and as it soared above the crowd its long tail swished behind it. The worst part, though, was the bird's massive beak, which ended in a point sharp enough to pierce a man's skull.

And that was exactly what it did.

The bird dove into the crowd and a scream of pain ripped through the air. Then it was flying again, soaring away from the city with a man's body dangling from its beak. Blood dripped down on me as the bird flew over, its tail swishing at my head, and I ducked instinctively, but it was a worthless gesture. The grizzard had already disappeared.

"Are there more?" I asked no one in particular.

A man at my side, a Huni whose face and ears were pierced with dozens of teeth and claws, called back, "There will be. We must run."

A beat later, the siren sounded.

After that it was a wave of chaos as people charged down the street, screaming and running. Another grizzard appeared, diving into the crowd, and carried a woman off who was still twitching even as she disappeared from sight. I ran, desperately trying to keep up with the crowd, but I had no idea what to do or where I would be safest. I had never been outside during an attack before, and there were still three streets separating me from Saffron's house. I was unsure if I should keep running or try to hide in an alley when I came to one. They were typically narrow, probably much too small for the large birds, and might protect me, only I did not know when I would come upon the next one.

The crowd pushed me forward, and as I ran I caught sight of a few Fortis men wielding spears. The streets were so tight that I had no idea how they would ever manage to take the birds out, but for the first time ever, I was happy to see them.

I managed to make it to Saffron's street but safety was still more than ten houses away. The crowd had thinned as people ducked into homes and buildings and other places I was unfamiliar with, and with each passing second I felt more and more exposed. The grizzards were still flying over the city, I could hear their shrieks, but none were in view as I ran, and I had to hold onto the hope that it would stay that way.

So I kept running, sweating and out of breath, I pumped

my legs harder and harder, my skirts swirling around me with each step. My legs got tangled in them and I stumbled, letting out a cry of frustration when it happened. I managed to stop myself from falling, but the relief was short lived. Only a few steps later it happened again, and this time there was nothing I could do.

I hit the ground so hard that it knocked the air out of me. The bread I had been clinging to was smashed under my body and my wrist throbbed from hitting the pavement when I tried to brace myself from the fall. People ran past me, but I was trembling and disoriented for a moment, and I was still down when fresh cries rang through the air around me.

The shadow of the large bird moved over the street, heading right toward me. I pushed myself back on instinct, but only got as far as the wall. There was nowhere to go, and getting up right now would only mean drawing attention to myself. Plus, to get back to Saffron's house I would be forced to run toward the grizzard. So I stayed down, praying that the bird would fly over me.

It swung its neck toward me as it flew. The bird's eyes were a bright yellow that looked unnatural against the black feathers, and when they zeroed in on me, I knew it. I put my hands up, trying to cover my head in hopes that it would do something to protect me, but deep down I knew there was nothing I could do to change what was about to happen.

The bird was right in front of me when it opened its beak and let out a shriek. I barely had time to blink before it slammed into me. The impact knocked me on my back, and I swung my arms and legs wildly, trying to knock the animal off, but it refused to give. I braced myself for the pain I was certain would come, but it never did. The bird's beak never pierced my body, it did not lift me into the air and fly away, it never even moved.

As suddenly as when it had slammed into me, the corpse was ripped away and I was set free. Rays of sunlight shone down through the buildings, blinding me when I looked up, but they were blocked a second later when Asa stepped in front of me.

"Indra." He knelt and the sun once again blinded me. "Are you okay?"

I held my hand up to shield my eyes and found him looking me over. He acted as if he wanted nothing more than to pick me up and carry me to safety, but he stayed where he was. He held a spear in his hand, the tip of it stained red, and I realized that he had saved me yet again.

"I am okay," I gasped.

Asa's head dipped once before he looked back over his shoulder. "The way is clear now, but the birds are still attacking. Come with me and I'll get you back to the house safely."

I pushed myself up off the ground, taking the loaves of bread with me even though I knew they were ruined. Asa only looked my way once before charging down the street, and I ran after him, staying close. The shrieks of the birds echoed all over the city and every other Outlier had now taken cover, leaving room for the Fortis to do their jobs. Eight houses away a group of them charged toward a bird as it swooped down, spears flying as they went. One hit home and the grizzard careened to the right, slamming into the wall at its side in a burst of feathers and shrieks.

Asa turned into the alley that ran beside Saffron's house and I followed, and only moments later he was shoving the door to her house open.

I took one step through, but paused so I could turn to face him. "Thank you."

His intense brown eyes held mine for a split second before he gave me a quick nod, and then he turned and ran back out into the street.

SIXTEEN

MY WRIST WAS MORE INJURED THAN I HAD originally thought. Adrenaline had kept me from feeling the pain right away, but after I returned to the house and Mira helped me clean up, it began to throb. Even though Saffron was not pleased that I had smashed the bread, she had chosen not to punish me in light of the grizzard attack. She did inform me that I would need to return to the bakery as soon as the streets had been cleared, though.

"She cannot send you out after this," Mira said as soon as Saffron left the room.

"The streets will be fine by then," I told her. "Safer even. The Fortis will be busy cleaning up the birds."

"They will have a feast tonight," Mira said grudgingly.

"Yes," I replied, unable to keep some of the same bitterness from my voice.

Grizzard attacks happened often, which was exactly why so many Fortis guards were employed inside the walls of the city. The birds traveled in flocks that sometimes numbered in the hundreds, and their attacks were usually spread out evenly between the Fortis village and Sovereign City. After it was over the carcasses were collected and taken outside the walls, which meant the Fortis were free to claim them. On those days even the walls were unable to keep the smell of roasting meat out.

True to her word, Saffron ordered me back to the bakery as soon as the siren had sounded, giving the city the all clear. The streets felt empty when I headed out. The usual crowds were still cowering in buildings, and the shrieks of the grizzards had all been quieted. The road that ran in front of Saffron's house was empty of people, but there were at least half a dozen dead birds lying on the ground. I hurried by the one that Asa had killed, shivering when I remembered the moment its cold, yellow eyes had zeroed in on me. In that instant, I had been certain it was going to kill me. As usual though, Asa had arrived just in time to save me, and I could not help thinking that I would never stop being indebted to him. There was nothing I could do to pay him back for all he had done for both Mira and me, because I was just an Outlier. I had no power. I was nothing.

With the exception of the same Huni woman who had been behind the counter the first time I was here, the bakery was empty. The electric lights shone down from above, highlighting every ridge on the woman's shaved head, and the eyes that looked me over were the same shade of sandy brown as her skin.

"You look like you had a close call," she said.

"I did."

She glanced beyond me, toward the street. "They come into our village sometimes. My mother was killed by one of them when I was a little girl. Their shrieks haunt my nights."

"I am sorry."

The woman tore her eyes from the door barely blinking before she said, "She was a great hunter and had many lovers. She lived an honorable life and she died an honorable death."

"It sounds like it," I replied, unsure of how else to reply.

The Huni intimidated me more than any of the other Outlier tribes because their customs were so opposite of ours. The women were treated as if they were as strong as the men, and they did not believe in monogamy. It made it difficult, if not impossible, to know how to interact with them.

"Be careful on your way back," the woman behind the counter said when she held the bread out to me.

"Thank you," I replied as I took the bread from her, "I will."

More and more people appeared in the streets as I headed home. The Fortis were hard at work clearing the bodies and cleaning the blood from the pavement, and I began to worry that Asa might not be back by the time Mira and I were ready to leave. When I turned back into the alley that led to Saffron's house, he was already there. Waiting for me.

"Mira said you were hurt." His gaze moved to my wrist, but he made no move to touch me. Which I was grateful for.

"I will be fine. Thanks to you."

The urge to say more came over me, the words tickling my tongue as they tried to get out, but I bit them back. I could not tell this man—a man I was not married to—that I was indebted to him. Even if it was the truth. It would change our relationship, put me in a situation where everything would be added to the list of things I could never repay him for.

Of course, if I acknowledged the truth to myself, I would have to admit that it was already that way. At least on my side. Figuring out what was going through Asa's head was impossible though, because he was impossible to read.

Instead of telling him all the things I had been thinking, I nodded to the door. "I need to get this bread to the kitchen so Mira and I can leave."

His head dipped when he nodded. "I'm right behind you."

We repeated our normal end of the day routine, Asa pretending he searched us before he made certain that we got out of the city safely, and more than any other day I found myself watching him as we went through the motions, wondering what he was thinking and more than anything, what his motivation behind it all was. They were questions I would never have the answers to, but it was impossible to banish them from my mind after such an eventful day.

By the time we made it through the gate, the scent of roasting bird was overwhelming enough to make my legs weak. Asa escorted us through the village as usual, but for the first time we met very little resistance. It seemed that everyone was busy either preparing the birds or working on the quarters being built for the Outliers. Something I had forgotten about in the midst of the grizzard attack.

Like always, Asa stopped at the threshold of his village and Mira and I continued on alone, and like always the Fortis man watched us walk away in silence. With each passing day, I found the quiet way he went about life less and less unsettling. In fact, there was something almost relaxing about it.

"What are we going to do about that?" Mira asked when we stopped to retrieve our weapons.

I glanced back once under the pretense of looking at the construction now well under way, but instead focused on Asa, who was now headed back to his village. "I don't know."

My gaze was torn from the man who had saved me when Mira tapped my bow against my arm. She had retrieved our weapons and replaced the rock, and was now waiting for me so we could head home. The knowing look on her face told me she knew that I had not been looking at the building. A flush spread across my cheeks and I turned my back to the village as I took the bow and arrows from her, slinging them over my shoulder. Then we started walking.

With the pounding of the hammers fading in the distance, the silence between us felt heavy. Earlier today I had begun to reconsider Bodhi's proposition that we head out into the wastelands, but walking beside them now, with the shadow of the grizzard attack hanging over us, I once again felt the impossibility of the plan. It was about more than just my mother's health. It was about Anja and how we would be ripping her away from the village just as she was getting close to Jax. It would be about leaving Mira behind, and Bodhi's family too. He had not thought it all through, and I needed to do it for him.

"How is your wrist?" Mira asked.

A stifling breeze blew across our path, bringing with it dust from the wastelands, and I covered my eyes. "It will be fine. I am more concerned with how Bodhi is going to react."

"You are lucky, Indra."

"I know." I glanced at her without turning my face. "There is much more to it than that."

Mira's brows lifted, but she said nothing, instead waiting for me to tell her on my own. In the light of what had transpired, I found myself wondering if she thought I was referring to Asa, and it was that possibility which finally made me decide to let Mira in on everything that had been happening in my life.

I first relayed what Bodhi and I had seen in the wastelands beyond the cave, and then what we had learned about the tunnel behind Sovereign City and the baby that Xandra had brought back to the village. After that it spilled out of me. I told Mira all of it, everything I had been keeping to myself, and I found that it was a relief to share my worries with someone. It should have been Bodhi, I should have been able to let him ease my anxiety, but the fear of what would happen if I did stopped me.

"You cannot tell Bodhi about Asa," Mira said firmly when I had stopped talking.

For the first time since this had all started I felt like she understood why I was so quick to keep Asa a secret, and I was more grateful than ever that I had decided to tell her.

"I know."

"You cannot leave either, Indra. You must know that."

"I do. It was a nice dream, but that is all it is. If there was something beyond the wastelands, I think we would know about it after all these centuries."

"Maybe," Mira said, "but even if it exists, you cannot possibly survive trying to reach it. They are called the wastelands for a reason. Nothing grows. There is no water. You bake during the day and freeze at night. Bodhi does not understand. He is smart, but he has not come out here as much as we have. He has never seen how far the wastelands go."

She was right. Bodhi had only seen the never-ending desert from a distance. Not like Mira and me, who traveled the borderland between the Lygan Cliffs and the wastelands on a daily basis. Bodhi did not see the dangers we saw, he had never felt the dread they could bring. If we went beyond what we knew, to the ruins or further, it would be even worse. There could be creatures out there that were twice as dangerous as the ones we knew, I was certain of it.

No matter what the Sovereign brought down on us, it had to be better than what was out there.

MY HUSBAND HAD NOT YET RETURNED FROM THE forest when Mira and I reached our village, something that happened only when his day of hunting had yielded very large game, and even after I had changed into my own clothes he had still not found his way back to me. Having nothing else to do, I decided to take the opportunity to visit with my mother.

She was asleep when I slipped into the hut, and all it took was one glimpse at her face for me to feel as if I had been pulled back in time. I was once again a small girl, and all I wanted to do was curl up beside her on the bed. As surely as if I were there at this moment, I could feel the rough skin of her fingers as they stroked my arm, the skin on her hands dry and cracked from washing dishes in Saffron's house, but comforting anyway because they were familiar. I longed to be that girl again, to have fewer responsibilities on my own shoulders, but I knew there was no going back, and I also knew that my mother was too weak to carry the burden. I was the adult now, the passage markings on my temples proved it. Both my mother and Anja needed me, and I owed it to them to push aside silly notions about running away and instead focus on what I needed to do inside the city to ensure that my family had the things they needed.

Careful not to wake my mother, I lowered myself onto the floor beside her thin mattress. Her face was relaxed, but even with the extra game Bodhi had provided, she seemed to have lost more weight. I was well aware that her time was getting shorter every day, a fact that no amount of medicine from Sovereign City could change. Since getting married I had found less and less free time to spend with her, and as I stared at her thin frame now, I chastised myself for being so selfish. She had taken me in when I had no one, raised me and trained me to take her place in the city. I owed her everything, but over the last couple months I had neglected my duties. It was something that needed to change.

My mother stirred, and with her eyes still closed reached out to find my hand. Her skin was no longer as dry as it had once been, but her hands were bonier, foreign.

She turned her head my way and opened her eyes. "Do not make yourself feel bad, child."

"What do you mean?" I scooted closer and her fingers flexed on mine, giving them a reassuring squeeze.

"I know you, Indra. You are feeling guilty that you cannot be here more. Are you not?" I nodded, and she gave my hand another squeeze, this one weaker than the last. "Do not trouble yourself. You have a husband to attend to and I sleep most of the time now. Things have changed, and I will not allow you to take on blame where there is none."

Her words seemed to sink into me. Instead of making me feel better, they caused a lump to form in my throat. "I should try to come more," I said in a gravelly whisper.

"You come enough." She glanced down to our entwined hands and her mouth pulled down in the corner. "What happened to your wrist?"

"There was a grizzard attack in the city today."

She shook her head ever so slightly. "I do not miss those birds."

"I was out. On the street." I paused and swallowed when the memory of the large bird's yellow eyes made me shiver. "It was a close call, but a Fortis guard managed to take the bird out before it got me."

"At least they are good for something."

She let out a deep sigh and her eyes once again slipped shut, but her grip on my hand remained firm. I stayed quiet, thinking that she might be once again drifting off to sleep and not wanting to disturb her if rest was what she required.

Her eyes were still closed when she said, "I miss the city, sometimes. Not the work or the Sovereign, and especially not the Fortis, but the beauty of it all."

Beauty? I had never looked at much of anything in the city as beautiful, at least not after the first week or two of working there, and especially not lately. True, in the beginning I had marveled at the chandelier and the homes that were solid and tall, towering over my head. I had stared in awe at the paintings hanging in Saffron's house. Pictures of gardens that were more colorful than even the wilds, and bodies of water that stretched out the way the wastelands did now. But those things had lost their charm, and now they seemed as useless and impractical as the Sovereign themselves.

"It's hard to see at times," my mother continued without opening her eyes, "but there is so much beauty that we take for granted. In the wastelands and the Lygan Cliffs, even in the creatures that live there." Her eyes opened to slits and focused on me. "They have adapted and found a home in a place where nothing should be able to live. Even better, they have thrived. Just as we have."

"What do you mean?"

"The Sovereign have spent centuries trying to keep the Outliers down, but we have not given up, have not let them win. Instead, we have figured out a way to survive, and we outnumber them. We are stronger than we believe ourselves to be, Indra. Always remember that."

I found myself unable to utter a sound. My mother was a strong woman, this was something I had always known. She had taken on the responsibility of keeping Anja and myself fed after our father's death, and she had done it without a complaint. But she was still an Outlier and a woman, two things that should have worked against her in this world. Inside the city walls we were looked at as lower than animals, and in our village we were told time and time again that we were weak and needed to be protected. And yet, looking at my mother now, she acted as if she did not believe any of those things. The opposite, actually. Even as sickly and weak as she was right now, the expression in her eyes made her look fierce and strong.

"I do not believe that I am strong," I said.

"You have fought off lygan attacks." Her fingers tightened on mine, showing that she had more strength left in her than I had originally thought. "You have faced people who violated you."

My cheeks flushed at the memory of Lysander and I wanted to look away, but I found it impossible. It was as if my mother's gaze had captured mine.

"I had to," I whispered. "If I did not, you and Anja would have suffered."

"That is strength, Indra. Being able to stand tall when the world wants nothing but to pound you to dust. *That. Is. Strength.* Remember that." Her grip on my hand eased and her body relaxed, and a beat later her eyes were once again closed. "It is something you can not afford to forget. Not when the world is as uncertain as it is. If I had been unaware of my strength when your father died, we would have starved."

I kept my hand in hers. In no time at all her breathing had deepened and her body had gone completely slack. I knew that she needed the rest, but I found myself wishing she were still awake. Her words were still spinning around in my head, and I was trying desperately to grab hold of them, but after a lifetime of being told I was nothing, it was a difficult thing to do.

Even though the things my mother had said were true, I could not feel strong. Facing a lygan was a matter of survival. If I had not stood my ground, the thing would have ripped me to shreds. It did not mean I was strong, only that I had no desire to die. It was different with the Sovereign and Fortis. Looking the other way when they hurt others, enduring the abuse they flung at me, that was how I would survive inside the city walls. Fighting back was unrealistic and would only get me killed.

JUST LIKE THE DAY THAT MIRA AND I ENCOUNTERED the lygan, Bodhi saw that I was injured the second he set foot in our hut that night.

"Indra." He took my hand gingerly in his, staring at my wrist with an expression that made him look as if he were in physical pain. "What happened? Who did this to you?"

"No one, calm yourself," I said gently. "There was a grizzard attack today, and I fell trying to get away. I am fine."

His shoulders relaxed even though concern still swam in his eyes. "It looks swollen."

"It barely hurts." I pried my wrist from his hands. "Did you get something big?"

"A boar." He straightened his shoulders the way he always did when he was proud of something he had accomplished. "A big one."

I wrinkled my nose at the thought of the round, flat-nosed creatures with the pointed tusks that could gore a man all the way through. They were a treat when cooked, especially as rare as they were this far from the lake, but they were mean and smelled worse than the dung building at the edge of our village.

Bodhi was watching me though, and the expectation shimmering in his eyes made a smile curl up my lips. I knew what he was waiting for, and I had no desire to disappoint him.

I stood on the tips of my toes and kissed him gently, whispering, "Thank you for providing for me. "

His smile grew and he seemed to stand taller at my words. My husband may have seen me as strong enough to hunt, and he may have said that women could take care of themselves if necessary, but he was still Winta, and in our tribe men prided themselves on being able to take care of their women. Bodhi was no different.

SEVENTEEN

LYSANDER'S WEDDING DAY ARRIVED AT LAST, and it was a flurry of activity from the moment I stepped into the house to the moment I left to return home. Not that I had expected anything less. The actual ceremony was held in the community building, a lavish event that all the Sovereign were invited to, but the feast that followed was held in the house and would be attended by only the elite.

Under the watchful eye of the Fortis guards, the other Outliers and I worked tirelessly to prepare the food and ready the home while the family was attending the ceremony. All the normal chores had been put aside for the day, allowing us to dedicate every moment to the event. Saffron's expectations where high, and we all knew that if they were not met the punishment would be severe.

My head was down, focused on the task of arranging the plates on the table when a grunt caught my attention and I lifted my gaze. Across the room, Asa was rubbing his arm as another Fortis guard leaned into him, putting his face so close to Asa's that not even my hand would have been able to fit between them.

"Watch where you're going," the man snarled. "Outlier lover."

Asa flinched away, but said nothing in response, and my own body stiffened. I was uncertain if the anger that shot through me was for him or for myself.

The Fortis guard let out a snort and once again Asa's head jerked back.

"Nothing to say for yourself, huh?" His eyes flicked down and his lip curled up in disgust. "You're a disgrace to your people. A traitor who isn't fit to shit in the same outhouse as the Fortis, let alone wear the uniform." He moved closer and this time his nose pressed against Asa's cheek. "Watch yourself."

Asa still hadn't said a word when the man stepped back, but his entire body tensed when the other guard glanced my way. He was quiet for a moment, looking me over. Thoughtful. Then he smiled, only the expression had no joy in it. It was all rage. All disgust.

"Maybe you're onto something," he snarled. "Maybe I'll take her for a ride, see what's special about Outlier pussy."

This time when Asa jerked, his eyes darkened as he curled his hands into fists. I expected him to lunge at the other man, but he stayed still. Instead, he said something in a voice much too low for me to catch a single word. Whatever it was, it made the other guard roar with laughter.

"Watch your back, Asa," the man said just before turning away.

Asa's gaze followed the other guard until he had slipped out of the room, and then his eyes were on me. The expression in them softened and the hair on my scalp prickled. Again he said nothing. There was nothing he could say, not out in the open like this. Not where anyone could hear.

I continued with my work, but it was impossible to forget what I had witnessed. It stayed with me the rest of the day, as I served wine for Saffron's guests, as I cleared dirty dishes, as I washed them. I had always known what Asa was risking by helping me, and before now it had been possible to convince myself that his efforts had gone mostly unnoticed. Other than the altercation with Thorin after Ronan's hand was cut off, I had seen nothing to indicate that the other guards knew what was happening. I had been wrong. The guard from the dining room knew, and if he knew, others did as well. I was causing problems for Asa that had nothing to do with the Sovereign. Problems that would follow him out of the city and leave him vulnerable.

I wanted to talk to him, but getting a moment alone with a Fortis guard was no easy feat. Especially once the family and other guests returned to the house, ready to celebrate Lysander's union. The groom was already drunk, as was his father, and the bride did nothing but stand in the corner at her mother's side while Paizlee bragged about the joining of the two houses.

I did everything I could to avoid Lysander as I poured wine, and other than a moment when he snuck up behind me and grabbed my backside, I was successful. Unfortunately, not everyone in the house was so lucky. The house was so crowded that none of the guests noticed when he slipped into the kitchen. Being in the main part of the house meant I had no idea who he had cornered. With Mira on the other side of the room and safe from his clutches, all I could do was say a quiet prayer that he was quick.

Lysander was gone for only fifteen minutes, but the smug expression on his face when he reemerged from the kitchen told me all I needed to know.

Even with the little distraction Lysander had provided, I found it impossible to forget the interaction between Asa and the other guard. The guests drank and I poured wine, moving about the room and doing everything in my power to avoid looking toward the man who was constantly on my mind.

It was more than halfway through the day before I finally managed to squeeze in a moment of private conversation. I had moved on from pouring drinks to collecting empty wine glasses from around the room when I paused next to him.

"I am causing trouble for you," I said in a voice just loud enough for Asa to hear.

My back was to him as I pretended to wipe the table the glass had been sitting on, so I was unable to see his expression, but I could picture it. The way he looked at me, with his feelings so raw and open, was etched into my mind at this point.

"I'm causing trouble for myself," he replied.

I ventured a glance his way. He was staring across the room, and the expression on his face was exactly as I had imagined it, only there was something else too. Pain.

Before he could catch me looking, I turned my gaze back to the table. "I am sorry."

"There's nothing to be sorry for, Indra."

My heart constricted at the sound of my name on his lips. Just like it always did, and before I could say anything else, I hurried back to the kitchen with the empty glasses of wine I had collected.

ASA WAS ESPECIALLY QUIET THAT NIGHT AS HE escorted Mira and me through the city, and then through his village. During this part of the journey, I typically kept my head down, wishing to avoid making eye contact with any of the Fortis. This time I forced myself to look around and take note of the people we passed. Some ignored us, but the majority of the men and women stared at us openly as we walked by. Many of them had the same expression of disgust I was used to seeing on the faces of the Fortis, a hatred for me simply because I was an Outlier. More than a few were focused on Asa though, and the rage in their eyes was something I had never witnessed before. At least not until earlier when the other guard had confronted Asa.

Today when he stopped at the edge of his village, I turned to face him instead of continuing on. "Will you be okay?"

At my side, Mira shifted, and I could feel her gaze on me, but I kept my focus on Asa.

"Greer has never liked me. Nothing can change that."

He was a man of few words, but after all these months I had learned to read between his words and get to the root of what he was really saying to me.

"You have always been on the outside with your people?"

"Yes," he said quietly, "but I'm not alone. I have friends. People who will be on my side against men like Greer."

My gaze moved beyond him, back toward the Fortis village and the rough men and women who lived there. The place was a cesspool, a collection of stink and misery, and I was unsurprised to learn that Asa did not fit in with these people. It was a shock to learn that there were others, though. Were there other men and women living in those shacks that would put their necks on the line for me? Were they helping other Outliers as Asa was helping me? I had always assumed that his feelings for me were responsible for the risks he took. Maybe I was wrong. Maybe whatever he felt for me was only partly responsible. Maybe it was simply his humanity.

"Be careful, Asa," I said, pulling my gaze away from the village and focusing on him.

That same expression was in his eyes, the one that told me without words how he felt, but for once it did not make me uneasy. Instead, I saw it for what it was. Proof that there was goodness even in the most unlikely places. Proof that no matter how different, people could work together.

Asa dipped his head twice, his eyes on me the whole time, and then he turned and headed back into his village.

When he had gone, Mira and I turned as well and headed for the rock that concealed our weapons. She was silent, thoughtful, but it only lasted until we were both armed.

"You care for him." There was no judgment in her eyes when she looked at me, and I found it impossible to even judge myself.

"I do." I turned to look back toward the village. "Not in the way that I care for Bodhi—I do not love Asa—but I do care for him."

"It would be impossible not to after everything he has done," she said.

"Yes," I replied.

We stood in silence for a moment, and then my eyes strayed from the village to the quarters the Fortis were busy building. Not much had changed over the last few weeks, and little more than a frame was done. At this rate, it would take them years to finish the building.

I nodded to the quarters. "The Fortis are moving slowly."

"Lucky for us," Mira said with a sigh.

"What will you do when it is done?"

She turned her back on the Fortis village and started walking, and I followed her lead.

"I do not know," Mira said. "I cannot stomach the idea of being a slave to the Sovereign, and if I move there that is what I will be. What about you?"

"It pains me to say it, to think about giving up the medicine and other supplies the Sovereign give us, but I will have to quit. I am married, and I cannot leave Bodhi." A lump rose in my throat at the thought of it. "I cannot imagine living without him."

Mira shook her head. "Leaving him would be impossible."

"Yes," I murmured.

SINCE THE DAY OF THE GRIZZARD ATTACK, I HAD been trying to visit my mother more and more, and I was fortunate enough that my husband joined me in the effort. That evening, after I had returned home and changed into my own clothes, Bodhi and I ate with my mother and Anja in their hut.

It was a quiet affair, as visits with my family usually were. Even with the added presence of Jax, who Anja had begun spending more and more time with. My sister was a woman now, even if it was difficult for me to imagine her as anything but a five-year-old girl who had refused to walk across the village unless she was holding my hand, and I knew that it would not be long before she was also a married woman. Based on the way our mother looked between her youngest daughter and Jax, she knew it as well.

After we ate, the four of us left the hut so our mother could rest. Like Anja, Jax was tall and slim, all wiry muscles like most Outliers. Walking beside them made me feel like a child, and I had to remind myself that I was six years older than my sister.

The two men discussed their day of hunting while Anja and I slowed until we walked a few steps behind them.

"Jax has been over a lot," I said, giving my sister a knowing look.

"He has." Her head dipped as if she was trying to hide her smile from me. Being that I was so much shorter than her, it was easily visible.

"Have you talked about the future?"

Anja nodded, but then shrugged immediately afterward. "Yes. But mother is so sick…"

"Anja." I stopped walking and grabbed my sister's arm. "She does not want you to put your life on hold. The opposite. She wants to be able to see you living it while she is still alive."

My sister swallowed and looked away. "I know."

"What is holding you back?" I asked when she refused to meet my gaze.

Anja looked up, and she had just opened her mouth when a scream broke through the air.

I turned toward the sound, my hand still on Anja's arm, but saw nothing. Bodhi and Jax were far ahead of us now, and there were more than two huts separating us. Another shout echoed through the night as the two men turned our way, and their eyes were filled with terror. I still had a grip on Anja's arm and it trembled in my grasp as more yelling followed the last cry.

Bodhi took one step toward me, ripping his knife out as he did, but his path was cut off when a forest cat jumped from between the huts. Its fur was white, making it stand out against the dark night, and when it opened its mouth, the light from the surrounding fires glinted off its teeth. A roar broke through the crowd, drowning out the screams and causing the hair on my arms to stand up.

Beyond the cat, Bodhi and Jax were both armed, but Anja and I were defenseless. As were all the other women in the village.

The cat's head rolled our way when I jerked my sister back. It roared again, and at my side Anja whimpered. Just as I had with Isa when I was facing Thorin in the Fortis village, I pushed my sister behind me, putting myself between danger and the weaker person. We were both unprotected against the cat, but I had faced creatures before. Anja had lived a sheltered life in the village.

Even though I was not focused on him, I saw it when Bodhi's eyes grew large. He headed for me just as the cat did, both of them running as if their lives depended on reaching their target. Behind me Anja shrieked again, and I pushed her down, lowering myself as well so my body was curled over hers. My name rang through the air, but I did not lift my head to look at Bodhi. Did not look back to see how close the cat was. I could only focus on my sister. On keeping her safe.

Another roar sounded, this time so close I felt the animal's breath. My body tensed and I held my sister tighter, waiting just as I had with the grizzard, but the creature never reached me. A moment passed where I stayed frozen, hovering over Anja with my heart pounding, and then I finally lifted my head.

Bodhi stood over me, the cat motionless at his feet. His shoulders rose and fell as he gasped for breath, but his eyes were on me. It sent me back to that moment in the city when Asa had saved me from the grizzard, and instead of making me feel grateful to the man who had saved me, the man who had vowed to protect me and provide for me, it made me feel useless. Weak and silly. Nothing but a Winta woman.

"Indra." Bodhi was on his knees next to me in a moment. "Are you okay?"

I released my sister and allowed my husband to pull me in for a hug. Anja was crying, and it was only a moment later that she was in Jax's arms as well.

No tears came to my eyes, and I did not even try to reassure Bodhi that I was okay, because I was too busy looking past him. All across the village scenes identical to ours were playing out. Women cowering in fear as their men killed the other cats in the pack. Women unarmed. Women defenseless and useless.

"Indra," Bodhi said again.

I tore my eyes from the scene and focused on him.

"Are you okay?

"Yes," I finally said, but I was pretty sure it was a lie.

I was not okay. I was outraged. I felt robbed of all my strength and dignity. Bodhi had lifted me up by taking me into the forest, but it had all been fake. A mirage. Back in the village, I was still just a woman. And that was all I would ever be.

EIGHTEEN

E VEN AS EARLY IN THE DAY AS IT WAS, THE sun was doing its best to bake Mira and me on our way to work. Summer, like spring, had come early this year, and I could not help feeling that it was a sign of things to come. A sign that the crops would have more trouble growing, that their fruit would be less bountiful, and that the rare rain we got would be scarcer this summer than ever before. Even worse was the fact that the excessive heat seemed to rile the lygan up, and three times that morning Mira and I were forced to take defensive positions when we heard the click of their claws against the rocks. Fortunately for us, the creatures never made an appearance and we managed to make it beyond the cliffs unharmed.

By the time we reached Saffron's house, Mira and I were both sweating and exhausted. The day had not even started yet, but it did not take me long to realize that it was about to get much, much worse. Asa was not at his usual post.

It was the first thing I noticed after stepping into the living room. Lately he had been standing guard at the door — a fact that I took note of every morning upon arriving at the house — but on this particular day a guard whose name I did not know stood in Asa's place. Immediately, I knew. I could feel it all unraveling, could feel that I had reached some major crossroad in my life.

Something bad was about to happen.

If Mira noticed he was missing she said nothing about it. Not that there was anything to say. We had work to do, and that would not change simply because the man who had been watching over us for months was missing from work. Saffron did not care if we lived in fear, none of the Sovereign did. We were Outliers, and we were only as useful as the work we did inside the walls.

So I did as I was expected and went about my usual tasks, only for the first time ever I dreaded the end of the day. Each second was spent looking over my shoulder, imagining that every guard in the house was watching me, coming up with different ways to torture me. Counting down the minutes until they got their hands on me. It never occurred to me that they were not the men I should worry about. Not after everything that had happened over the last few months. Not after everything I had witnessed.

After my close call in the streets, Saffron had graciously restored me to my role as housemaid, but I had been given a different position. Now instead of preparing the family's meal, I usually found myself on cleaning duty. Cleaning the bathrooms or scrubbing the floors, or any other manual labor Saffron could conjure up, all jobs that were usually reserved for new servants. This meant that I had no idea two extra places had been set until the moment I stepped into the dining room for dinner service, and by then it was too late. He was already sitting at the table, and the look in Lysander's eyes as he surveyed the staff told me he was on the prowl.

Dinner was as tense as it always was when Lysander was around. Somehow, against all odds, Mira and I managed to make it through the meal without getting too close to him, and I found myself praying that our good fortune would last and we would make it out of the house unscathed. If we did, being stripped on our way out of the city might be the worst thing to happen. It would be humiliating, but nothing compared to what could happen inside these walls where no one would be the wiser.

The day came to an end, and Mira and I hurried to the mudroom in hopes of slipping out unnoticed, but someone was already waiting for us. Not Lysander, but Greer, the same guard I had seen giving Asa a hard time on Lysander's wedding day. Greer had been paying attention, I was certain of that, and he knew that Asa had been keeping an eye on us. When he failed to show up for his shift, Greer must have seen it as his lucky day.

"You know the drill," he growled when Mira and I stepped into the mudroom, the gleam in his eyes confirming that he had been looking forward to this for some time. "Clothes off."

Mira shot me a worried look, and I did my best to appear confident when I met her gaze. With my entire body shaking, I doubted she felt very comforted.

"It will be okay," I said as I reached for the buttons on my dress.

Mira followed my lead. My trembling fingers made it nearly impossible to get the tiny circles through the holes, and like me she seemed to be having the same problem. It was more than fear that made me tremble though. It was also fury. Fury at this man who saw my weakness as his to exploit, at the Sovereign who allowed it to happen, even at the other Outliers who did nothing to stop it. Most of all though, I was angry with myself for being too weak to resist. For being nothing but a woman.

"Hurry up," Greer snapped.

He stepped toward Mira, but my anger had given me courage, and I was there to cut him off, putting my body between the guard and my friend. The large man glared down at me, his dark eyes narrowing.

"I know the law," I said, trying to hold my ground despite the trembling in my legs. "You can search us, but you are not to touch us."

Surprise flickered in Greer's eyes. It was quickly replaced by rage that matched the fury surging through me. This had probably never happened before. Outliers never talked back; it was the same as asking for a beating. My sudden bravado was about more than finally standing up for myself. Right now, it was the only hope I had. I was certain that if I could just get Greer angry enough with me, he would leave Mira alone. She might be able to get out of the house. It was a long shot, but it was the only one we had.

Greer moved closer, so close that every breath I took filled my nostrils with his stink. "Is that—"

The door to the kitchen opened with a creak and he looked up. Behind me, footsteps entered the room and hope surged through me when Greer took a step back. It was Asa. It had to be. Somehow he had snuck into the house unnoticed and was here to save me yet again.

"I'll take it from here," Lysander said, the words coming out as smooth and malicious as butter laced with poison.

The sound of his voice pushed all my courage away. I would never be able to get away with defying *him*. Not without consequences at least.

"Sir," the guard in front of me began, "it's my duty—"

The hum of an electroprod filled the room and Greer's body reacted by jerking away from me.

"This is my mother's house," Lysander said as the electric hum grew louder, "therefore it's *my* duty."

Lysander's tone left no room for discussion even if the electroprod had, and after one quick glare at me, Greer was heading for the door. His footsteps felt as if they shook the entire house, but when the door clicked shut it seemed a hundred times louder.

Once we were alone, Lysander crossed the room to take the guard's place in front of me, his pudgy body so close I could feel the heat of him. He still held the electroprod in his hand, and my body involuntarily shrank away from the blue glow it gave off. It was rare that the weapons were used on Outliers since the Sovereign relied on the brute strength of the Fortis guards they employed, but it happened. I had seen it, more than once, and I had no desire to allow the electric shock of that rod to incapacitate me.

"Now, I believe you are to strip before you leave the house?" Lysander lifted his eyebrows as he looked back and forth between Mira and me. "We wouldn't want another incident of theft, now would we?"

His gaze focused on Mira, his eyes shimmering with something that made the hair on the back of my neck stand up. Already tears were streaming down my friend's face, but the sight of them did not rip me in half the way I thought they would. No, they fed the fury already building inside me, made my body shake with rage, made me think of everything we had endured. The oppression at the hands of the Fortis and Sovereign, the abuse. It was never enough for them either, because now they wanted to make those of us working in the city slaves, and once that happened the people in our villages would be left to starve. The meager help we got from the city would vanish, and soon my people would wither away until they were nothing more than memories. And then Outliers would be no more. They would be ghosts, just like the people who had lived in the old world.

It was too much to take. We took it anyway though, because no one had the courage to stand up to these people. No one ever fought back or said no, because the consequences were too great. Floggings and losing limbs, death, and the threat that much more could happen to our villages if we defied the Sovereign. No one could stop any of those things from happening, but I could stop this. Even if it meant facing punishment, I could stop Lysander from stealing from Mira what he had stolen from me three years ago.

"No," I hissed, the word pushing its way between my teeth like it was an animal trying to break free.

Lysander's eyes flicked my way just as I charged. I thought of nothing but Mira as I ran, gritting my teeth and propelling my body forward. My shoulder slammed into his round stomach and even though I was so much smaller than he was, I managed to catch him off guard. The electroprod fell to the floor and shut off when Lysander stumbled back. He slammed into the wall and then fell on the bench before landing right next to the weapon he had just dropped.

I spun to face Mira, my shoulders heaving from the anger surging through me, and the gulps of air I was forcing into my overworked lungs. "Go. Now. Run."

She only paused for a beat, staring at me with eyes that were wide and frightened, and then she spun on her heels and headed for the door.

Mira no doubt thought I would be right behind her, that I was doing this to save us both, and I did nothing to correct her. I knew the truth would make her hesitate, and that was the last thing I wanted. One of us should be able to get through this life unscathed, and since I already bore the scars of working in this house, that only left Mira.

I did follow her to the door, but there was no chance of me making it out. Even before I had thrown myself at Lysander I knew what was about to happen. I still screamed when his hand wrapped around my hair. He twisted my locks around his fingers and made a fist, jerking me back and forcing me to my knees, and then, with his eyes still on me, he kicked the door shut. Cutting off my only chance of escape.

"You must be out of your mind, Outlier. Do you know the punishment for hitting a Sovereign? Do you know what my mother will do to you?"

"Tell her," I growled, and then whimpered when he tightened his grip on my hair. Still, I managed to find my voice again so I could say, "Take me to her now. Tell her what I did. I will gladly accept my punishment, but I refuse to let you hurt my friend."

Lysander's sneer morphed into a smile that made his round face appear sick and sadistic. "I think I'll take on the responsibility of punishing you myself."

He jerked me up by the hair, forcing another cry from my lips, and then shoved me face-first against the wall. He had one hand on the back of my head, pressing my cheek against the wall while the other hand went for my skirt. His fingers brushed the bare flesh of my hips, and a second later he had a hold of my undergarments. When he pulled, they ripped from my body, and it seemed as if the sound was loud enough to drown out even my screams.

MY LEGS COULD BARELY HOLD ME UP WHEN I stumbled out of the house, and after only two steps I had to stop so I could lean against the wall. I was shaking, crying, hurting both inside and out, and all I wanted was to get home, but I had no idea how I would manage it.

"Indra." I jerked at the sound of my name, but had no

time to do anything else before Mira was at my side. "Are you okay? Tell me you are okay."

"I am fine," I lied.

Mira's fingers touched the underside of my chin, forcing me to meet her gaze. Her face was distorted from the tears shimmering in my eyes, but also because both my eyes were swollen and sore. Lysander had been serious when he said he would take my punishment upon himself. My right cheek throbbed just below my eye, and I was pretty sure that my bottom lip was bleeding. My left eye had made contact with the wall when he shoved me against it, and it felt as if it might swell shut, but those injuries were nothing compared to the ache in my wrists from being held down or the bruising that I knew would soon pop up on the inside of my thighs. The man had been brutal three years ago. That had been nothing compared to what he had done today. Those injuries I had been able to hide, but not these. What he had done was written all over my face in the form of cuts and bruises. The moment Bodhi laid eyes on me, he would know.

"Why?" Mira sobbed at my side. "Why did you do that? Why would you let him do that?"

There was nothing worse than having to comfort someone when you were the one hurting, but I knew Mira's tears were more about my pain than her own, so I did it anyway. "It is okay. I am okay." I tried to stand, but my legs were still shaking too much and I had to hold onto the wall for support. "Help me. I want to go home."

Mira swiped her hand across her face and did as I asked. She put her arm around my waist while I wrapped mine around her back, and together we headed for the gate.

Everyone we passed looked my way. Outliers with pity in their eyes, Fortis with a sickening gleam that said they thought I had gotten what I deserved, the Sovereign with looks of indifference that told me they did not care to what happened to people like me as long as their world was unaffected by it. The lines at the gate had gotten shorter and shorter with each passing day as the Fortis tired of their current game and moved onto other ways of torturing Outliers, and when the wall came into view, I was relieved to find only a few people waiting to get out.

The guard in charge put his hand up when we approached, but before he could say anything Mira snapped, "We have already been searched."

His gaze, cold and unsympathetic, moved over me briefly before he nodded and waved us forward.

The street outside the gate was surprisingly clear, which no doubt had to do with the fact that most of the Fortis were working on the quarters that would soon be filled with Outliers.

Mira tightened her grip on my waist and walked faster. "The worst part is almost over," she said as we moved through the village. "We will be there sooner than you think."

We had an hour walk ahead of us, but I grabbed hold of her words anyway, pretending they were true.

I scanned the faces that turned our way as we moved, wondering where Asa was, wondering what had happened to make him miss work today. I never saw him. Up until this point he had proven himself trustworthy, but I was unable to stop myself from wondering if he had turned his back on me.

He was a Fortis after all, and I was nothing but a dirty Outlier. No one, not even me, would be surprised if he decided I was unworthy of his protection.

"He must be sick," Mira said. "He never would have left you to fend for yourself unless something very bad had happened to him."

"He is a Fortis." The words came out as a grunt. "They have no honor."

She said nothing in response, but instead focusing on holding me up as we crossed out of the Fortis village and into the borderland.

We only paused once, to get our weapons, before continuing on. The walk through the borderland to the wilds was the longest one of my life, but the physical discomfort was only partly to blame. I knew everything would change the second Bodhi set eyes on me. He was already simmering with hate for the Sovereign, and with each step that brought me closer to home, I became more and more certain that no matter what I did, I would never be able to diffuse this situation. Too much had happened too fast, too much abuse had been piled on top of us too quickly. Not enough time had gone by between each incident to allow us to heal before something else was flung at us, and this would be like having a mountain of pain dropped on our village, on Bodhi. He would never recover from it, which meant neither would I.

I should have fled with him when I had the chance. It would have been better if we had both died in the wastelands than have to face this.

By the time the village came into view, I was barely on my feet, but I pushed myself, desperate to make it to my husband's comforting embrace. Then he was there, materializing from between the huts like he had known all along that this moment was coming. I burst into tears at the sight of him and my legs, which had been weak since the second I set foot outside Saffron's house, finally gave out. Mira let out a cry as I went down, trying and failing to hold onto me. There were shouts and calls for Adina, and then Bodhi was at my side, scooping me into his arms, his own tears mixing with mine as he carried me into the village.

NINETEEN

ODHI CARRIED ME TO OUR HUT AND STAYED at my side through the entire ordeal. Through Adina's examination of my injuries, her assurances that my womb had not been permanently affected, and then after when I got myself cleaned up. Mira stayed for a while too, her face streaked with tears and dirt from our trek through the borderland. Eventually, she was forced to return to her own hut even though I knew it tore her up to leave me.

Anja came and cried over me. Bodhi's mother came as well, bringing me the maternal comfort that my own mother was too sick to bring. For a while it seemed as if there was a never-ending flow of people coming in and out of our hut, and I was grateful for the company. Then, all at once, it stopped, and Bodhi and I were left alone.

He had said very little since lifting me into his arms, and I could feel the change boiling in the air around us. The heat of it made sleep impossible when I finally did lie down. At my side Bodhi was quiet, but his breathing told me that he too was awake. His silence terrified me. The longer it stretched out, the more difficult it became to figure out what to say to break it. I felt like no matter what I did I would only be throwing wood on a fire that was already threatening to swallow our entire village. Staying silent would give Bodhi's anger more time to simmer, but talking might force him over the edge.

Outside, the sun had set on the wilds and coated our hut in a blanket of black. It was the cover of darkness that finally gave me courage to break the silence, though. In the blackness of our hut, Bodhi would be unable to see the cuts and bruises on my face, would be unable to focus on the physical marks Lysander had left behind. If I could get my husband to listen to me, to really take in what I had to say, it just might save us all.

"You made a promise to me," I said to the dark figure at my side. "Do you remember?"

"I promised to protect you. Do you remember that?" Bodhi shifted so he was facing me, but he was little more than an outline. "Which promise would you have me break?"

"If you go into the city you will be breaking them both. Protecting me means being here, living, but if they catch you, they will put you to death. You cannot protect me if you are gone. How can you not see that?"

"I only see what they have done to you." He reached out and brushed his fingers down my face, over the cuts and bruises Lysander had given me.

I swallowed, almost too overcome with emotion to say

anything else, still knowing I had to get the words out. Had to make him understand.

"Then close your eyes and imagine what things would be like for me if you were gone. Do it." I found his hand in the darkness and gripped it, holding on tight, hoping the physical contact would help me get through to him. "Can you see it? Can you see how much it would hurt me? Can you see me crying myself to sleep? Can you see me starving because I am too broken to even try? That is what my future would be like if you did this."

Through the darkness of the room, I heard him swallow.

"Can you see it?" I said again, desperate to hear him tell me he understood.

"I can," he whispered.

"Then promise me that you will stay away from the city. Say it so I believe it. Tell me that you will never leave me."

"I promise," he said, moving closer to me, reaching out with his free hand so he could touch my cheek. "I promise that I will never leave you, Indra. I promise."

Through the darkness, his lips found mine. Even the gentle kiss made the cut on my bottom lip sting, but I pretended not to be in pain. We had spent enough time focusing on my pain today, and it was time to sleep.

I untangled my hand from his grasp and turned so my back was to his chest. Bodhi wrapped his arms around me, and some of the discomfort in my body eased.

"Sleep," I whispered into the darkness. "We will talk about it more when morning comes."

BODHI'S SIDE OF THE BED WAS EMPTY WHEN I WOKE, but I could tell by the bright light streaming in through the cracks around our door that I had slept much later than usual. He had gone hunting. That was all.

Hopefully in the forest he would be able to find some peace about what had happened.

I rolled onto my back and winced at the way my body throbbed. My lip felt like it was twice its normal size, but it seemed that neither one of my eyes had swollen as much as I had expected them to. Something I probably owed to Adina's healing touch.

Gingerly, I rolled out of bed. I still had to bite back a groan. There would be no work for me today, and maybe never again if it meant keeping Bodhi safe, but lying in the hut all day was out of the question. I would visit my mother so she could see with her own eyes that I was okay, and maybe go out into the forest with Bodhi later tonight. I needed to keep busy, to keep my focus on something other than what had happened to me, and that meant getting dressed and working through the pain.

I had just managed to wiggle my way into my clothes when the door to my hut was thrown open and Anja burst inside.

"Indra," she huffed out.

It only took one look at her wide eyes to know that something very bad had happened. "What? What is it?"

"Bodhi. He has gone to the city."

"No," I gasped, stumbling back but catching myself on the hut's support beam before my legs could give out.

Just last night Bodhi had promised me that he would stay away from the city, and when I had closed my eyes to go to sleep, I had felt certain that he had meant it. Then, only hours later, he had snuck out of our hut and done exactly what I had begged him not to do. He had left me.

"Are you sure?" I asked my sister, thinking she must be wrong. Praying that she was. He had to have gone hunting because there was no way Bodhi would do this to me. There was no way he would be this selfish.

But my sister nodded. "He left with Xandra."

Xandra.

The sound of her name felt like a punch. She was taking him to the tunnel, leading him into the city through the secret entrance. Why would she do this to me? How could she? Xandra had to know what this would mean for Bodhi, what it could mean for the entire village if the Sovereign decided they had had enough of the Outliers. This one act could be the end of us all.

I had to stop him.

I had already gotten dressed, but wearing my normal clothes would prevent me from getting into the city. My uniform would be necessary.

"How long ago?" I asked my sister as I began to undress.

"Less than an hour, I think."

Every move I made hurt, but it took no time at all for me to get out of my clothes, and then I was pulling my uniform dress on, trying not to think about the blood splattered across the sleeve or the painful rub of the fabric against my bruised skin.

"I need to hurry," I said, heading for the door, finding it impossible to ignore the way my inner thighs throbbed with each step I took.

Anja followed me out, keeping stride with me. "I just found out or I would have told you sooner."

"I have to get to him," I said, walking faster. "I have to get to Saffron's house before he does something stupid."

My sister hurried to keep up, gasping out, "I am coming with you."

I spun to face her, stopping her in her tracks. "No. You must stay here. Understand? I cannot risk anyone else." She opened her mouth to protest, but I cut her off when I grabbed her and pulled her against me. "I am serious, Anja. You must stay here. I need to know that you will be here to look after our mother if I do not make it back."

"If you do not make it back?" Anja pulled away so she could look me in the eye. "What do you mean?"

"The Sovereign will kill Bodhi if they catch him, and they may kill me just to make an example of us." I looked beyond my sister at the village, wondering if I should tell her the truth about what my husband's actions might cost all of us. When I looked back at her, I said, "If the Fortis show up and we have not made it back, I want you to take our mother and run. Understand?"

Anja's brown eyes grew to twice their size. "Where do I go?"

"Into the wilds. Stay away from the other villages. Going there would be too dangerous. You only need to hide until the Fortis are gone. Okay?" She nodded, and I pulled her in for another quick hug before turning away. "I have to go."

I had only taken two steps when Anja called after me, "Please come back, Indra. Promise me!"

I was unsure if it was a promise I could keep, so I said nothing and kept walking.

I HAD KNOWN THAT THE WALK TO THE CITY WOULD take longer than usual, but it seemed to stretch on forever. My body was more bruised than I had realized, and each step seemed to exacerbate the aches that radiated through me. Even worse, the sun was out in full force. It reflected off the sandy wastelands to my right and nearly blinded me all the while burning down on my head like it wanted to turn me to ash where I stood.

By the time the wall and Fortis village came into view, I was drenched in sweat and my body throbbed so much that every step took effort. I never slowed though, not once. I told myself that all I needed was to get to Saffron's house and then I would have help. Mira would be able to help me keep an eye out for Bodhi. Possibly Asa too, although my confidence in him was shaken thanks to the events of the previous day.

The Fortis village was alive with the pounding of hammers, but very few people were up this time of day. They slept late and stayed up even later, meaning most mornings we were able to get through with very little abuse thrown our way. Thankfully, today was no exception.

I made it through the gate to find the city buzzing with activity. It was late morning, a peak time for running chores, and the people crowded into the streets slowed me down and made it impossible to get very far without being jostled. The throng thinned out the closer I got to my destination, and by the time I made it to Saffron's street, the crowd was small enough that I could see all the way to the end of the road.

The house came into view and my already pounding heart beat faster. It only took one glimpse for me to realize that I was too late. A large group of Fortis guards were gathered in the street, right in front of Saffron's house, and there were even a few men and women I had never seen before going inside. I began to move faster, running on legs that threatened to give out, pushing myself with energy I should not have had.

I was still a whole house away from the crowd when Bodhi was dragged through the door. A trail of blood ran from his nose and his right eye matched mine, purple and nearly swollen shut, but he was still fighting.

"Bodhi!" The scream forced its way out of me as I pushed myself harder.

His head turned my way and he searched the crowd for me, but there were too many people separating us. Without thinking, I pushed past the guards gathered in the street, shoving men more than twice my size out of the way in my hurry to reach my husband.

"Indra!" Bodhi yelled when he finally saw me. He fought harder, earning him a shake from the guard at his back. "What are you doing here? Go home!"

I pushed one last man out of my way, and I had just reached Bodhi when my legs finally gave out. I dropped to my knees on the ground, sobbing at my husband's feet, desperate to get to him and throw my arms around him but too weak and exhausted to do it. Instead, I grabbed his legs and wrapped my arms around him.

"Why?" I sobbed. "You promised. You promised you would stay with me."

I doubted he could hear the words, but he had to know what I was saying. He had probably imagined the words coming out of my mouth his whole walk here, and yet he had come anyway. He had risked everything and lost, and now I was about to lose everything because of it.

"Get up, girl."

A boot made contact with my lower back and I cried out. My hands slipped from Bodhi's legs, and then he was gone, dragged from sight and swallowed up by burly bodies that stank of rage and sweat. Someone grabbed my arm and jerked me to my feet, and even though it hurt and I screamed, I was thankful for it. I needed to find Bodhi, only I was too weak to stand. The guard's grip was punishing, but I barely felt it as I searched the sea of men and women surrounding me, desperate for a glimpse of my husband.

When the back of his head came into view, his blond hair looking lighter than ever amongst the sea of dark clothes the Fortis wore, I almost burst into tears. He was being dragged away from the house, away from me, and the man holding me was pulling me in the other direction. I kept my eyes on my husband, watching until he had finally disappeared from view.

I gave up the second he was gone and allowed the man holding me to drag me forward. My feet tripped over one another the whole way, unable to find purchase or incapable of holding me up. I was unsure which one, but I also was unable to make myself care. All I knew was that everything was over. There was nothing left for me. Not anymore.

"You. Stop," someone called out. "This girl works in the House of Saffron."

The man holding me stopped and I nearly fell to the ground. "She caused a disturbance."

"You don't think Saffron can discipline her own Outliers?"

"Fine. Let her be your responsibility then," the guard holding me growled.

He shoved me forward and I slammed into a form that was as solid as a wall. I clung to it, knowing that I would fall if I let go, and to my surprise it took hold of me with hands that were so gentle they felt like a dream.

"It's okay," the man holding me whispered. "I have you."

When I looked up, I found myself face to face with Asa. He was looking me over, studying the cuts and bruises on my face, and the raw pain in his eyes mirrored the agony rolling through me.

He swallowed, but said nothing before scooping me up into his arms. He took me in through the housemaid entrance, into the mudroom that just yesterday had been the staging area for my destruction, and set me on the bench before kneeling in front of me.

Once we were face to face, I saw that I was not the only marked by violence. Asa had a cut on his cheek and bruises on his neck, as well as more cuts on his knuckles, and when he shifted, he winced as if he were in pain.

"What did they do to you?" I asked.

"Don't worry about me." He swallowed as if talking hurt, but I was unsure if it was physical or emotional pain. "I wasn't here to save you. It won't happen again."

"No one can save me now." I leaned my head back and stared at the ceiling.

We were both silent for a moment, and then Asa took my hands in his. The contact shocked me so much that I was forced to tear my gaze from the ceiling. He had never touched me before today, and carrying me inside had not really counted, not like this, because it had none of the intimacy that his warm, calloused hands on mine did. It should have felt like a violation, being in this room and having a man other than my husband touch me, but instead it achieved something that no one but Bodhi had ever been able to do. It comforted me.

"That was your husband?" Asa asked.

"It was."

"He came here to avenge you."

Asa's gaze went down. I knew he was not looking at our hands, which were still entwined in my lap, but at the bruises on my wrists. I wanted to pull away then. Not to avoid his touch, but to cover the marks that seemed to have Lysander's name written all over them.

"That was very brave of him," Asa said when he was once again looking me in the eye.

"Brave?" I shook my head. "He will die for what he has done."

"Maybe he couldn't live knowing he had done nothing."

"Maybe," I said.

Asa looked down again, only this time he *was* staring at our hands. My skin looked impossibly pale in his, like the first dusting of snow on the embers left behind by an evening fire, and the sight of it was a reminder of who we were. Of the two very different worlds we came from.

I pulled my hand from his, and he stood without so much as a blink. "I'll try to find out where they've taken him."

"Thank you," I whispered.

Asa avoided looking at me when he slipped from the room.

I WAS NOT ALONE FOR LONG. ONLY A FEW BEATS after Asa left, the door opened and Mira appeared before me. Her eyes were wet, her face twisted with pain. When she knelt in front of me, I found that I was surprisingly numb. It was as if I had already died. As if just seeing Bodhi in custody had been enough to take me out.

"Indra," Mira whispered.

She reached out to take my hand, just as Asa had only a short time ago, but I barely felt her touch. Not only that, I could think of nothing to say.

"Are you okay?" she asked when I said nothing.

I was only aware of the fact that I shook my head when my hair swished across my shoulders. "I tried to make it in time. I tried, but I could not save him."

Mira started crying again. "I am sorry. I am so sorry. I had no idea he was here until I heard yelling, and when I ran in he was already d-down. He—he was—"

Her words were lost in a tangle of sobs. It was unimportant, though. One day I would want to know what had happened, but right now I was unable to focus on anything.

The door behind Mira opened and a guard stuck his head in. Greer.

His mouth morphed into a grin when he saw me. "Mistress is looking for you." He shook his head. "Bet you wish I'd been the one in the room with you yesterday. Remember that next time and get your clothes off faster, no backtalk."

Mira wiped her face with the sleeve of her dress and glared at Greer.

Before she could say anything, I pulled my hand from hers and stood. "Go back to work, Mira. No one else needs to get into trouble today."

Greer followed me through the kitchen to the dining room, and then to Saffron's office. Even after I had stepped through the door he stayed close to me, and his presence on top of everything else made me feel as if my skin was covered in bugs.

Saffron was behind the desk, her electroprod sitting in front of her as usual, and a frown on her face that pulled her waxy skin tight.

She stood when I entered. "Indra."

Her gaze swept over me, and she visibly started. She must have suspected that there had been a confrontation between her son and myself last night, otherwise there would have been no way to explain why Bodhi had come here today, but she clearly had not known the extent of it.

She covered her surprise quickly, although not before glancing to her left. That was when I registered Lysander's presence. I kept my focus on his mother, but I knew he was watching me. I could feel his gaze on my face the same way I had felt the sun during the long walk here. It burned me.

"Mistress." I bowed my head, working to focus on the hardwood floor beneath my feet as Saffron walked closer.

"I understand your husband is the one who came into my house today?"

"So I have been told," I said.

"He attacked my son."

My gaze went from the floor to Lysander. He was lying on a couch like he was relaxing after a long battle, his own electroprod resting on his lap. Lysander's shirt was ripped and bloodied, revealing the soft paunch that he called a belly, and he had a bandage right above his right elbow, and another cut on his chest. Hopefully it got infected and he died.

I moved my gaze back to the floor. "I have been told that as well."

"That's all you have to say for yourself?" Saffron scoffed. "After everything I've done for your family?"

I lifted my eyes, daring to meet her gaze. "I was unaware that I was responsible for my husband's actions. Would you take on the responsibility for something your husband had done? Or your son?"

Anger flashed in Saffron's eyes. Any other day I would have shrank away from it, would never have dared to say anything like that to begin with, but I had nothing left to lose. Bodhi would die today, of that I was positive, and there was a strong possibility that I would as well. Just to teach the Outliers a lesson. Either way, I was unable to find the strength to hold back. Not anymore. Not knowing what they were about to do to me. What Saffron's family had already done to me.

"It is as much your responsibility as it is his," Saffron said through clenched teeth. "Because of the altercation *you* had with my son yesterday. There are consequences for your actions, Indra, something you are about to get a lesson in, and something you should have thought about last night before refusing to do your duty."

"You should have kept your mouth shut and let me search your friend," Lysander called from his position on the couch.

His mother waved him off, not taking her eyes off me. "I know you thought you were sticking up for your friend, but the law is the law, and no one is above it. Lysander was doing his duty."

"Would you stand by and watch your people be abused?" I asked Saffron. "Would you be able to do nothing while someone you loved was taken advantage of?"

Saffron stepped forward and slapped me. The sting of her palm against my cheek registered only because it forced my head back, but I felt very little pain from it. I should have. She had hit me right where my cheek had rubbed against the wall as Lysander violated me. For some reason though, it felt no more violent than a burst of wind blowing across my face.

"No, which is why both you and your husband will be punished today," Saffron said, her shoulders heaving with anger or adrenaline. "We cannot have anarchy in Sovereign City, and if Outliers like you aren't made an example of, that is what we will have. Your husband will be a warning to everyone who works in the city, and when he is dead, you will be taught a lesson as well."

She spun on her heel, her skirt swirling around her, and snapped her fingers. Immediately Greer was at my side, and his hand wrapped around my arm so tightly that it felt as if he were trying to squeeze it in half. Then I was pulled from the room.

TWENTY

FTER LEAVING SAFFRON, GREER LED ME through the winding streets of Sovereign City toward the center of town. His hand gripped my arm the entire way, and he walked so fast that I stumbled every few steps. With his hold on me, I never had a chance to fall. I was unable to really feel his grip, but I was with it just enough to know that it would hurt later, and that I would have a bruise there.

We reached the town square and my heart thumped harder. It was empty at the moment, but before long people would be crowded into it. People who had never spoken to my husband, but hated him just the same, each one of them eager to watch as Bodhi had his life stolen from him.

The raised platform that stood just in front of the government building overlooked the square. It was the very same platform I had stood on while Ronan had his hand cut off, and it held the same chairs that Saffron and her family had sat in that day. It was also were Greer dragged me now, up the steps and toward the door leading into the government building. My heart beat harder even though I knew my punishment had not yet arrived. The square was still empty, and if I were about to face my punishment, it would be brimming with people.

Instead of stopping on the stage, he pulled me inside the building and down a hall as gray and cold as the streets I walked down every day in this city. Doors made of thick, aged wood lined both sides of the hall, each one with a heavy padlock that told me they were for prisoners. No windows looked into the rooms, but I still found myself craning my neck in hopes of trying to discern which one held Bodhi. He was here somewhere, in this building at this very moment, and I knew it, but I also knew the Sovereign would never give me the chance to see him. It was unimportant to them whether or not I got to say goodbye to my husband.

Greer stopped in front of a door and when he pulled a ring of keys from his pocket, they clanged together and echoed down the silent hall. Only a moment passed before he had the cell open, and then I was shoved inside. I stumbled and fell to my knees on the cold stone, and I had just enough time to get a look around before the door slammed shut behind me.

I was plunged into darkness so thick that I was unable to see my hand when I held it in front of my face, but it was irrelevant. There was nothing in the room other than stone walls and a stone floor, so I curled up and hugged my knees to my chest, hoping to hold myself together. With the way I was trembling, I doubted I would be able to pull it off.

An indiscernible amount of time passed where I stayed in that position. My knees tucked against my chest, my arms hugging them as if they were the only things keeping me from cracking to pieces. The door was thick, but the pounding of footsteps still managed to penetrate it, and every time they drew near I found my body growing stiff as I waited to find out if this was the moment I was dreading. It happened over and over again until I began to wonder if they were teasing me. Playing a game in hopes of making me crack and crumble to pieces.

When the door was finally ripped open it came with no warning. Light flooded the room, making it impossible to see who was standing in front of me, and then two figures charged in. Though I tried to brace myself for what came next, I was still unprepared when they jerked me to my feet and I was dragged out into the cold hallway.

My eyes had almost completely adjusted to the light by the time I was pulled onto the stage. Greer and another guard whose name I did not know hauled me forward, each one gripping an arm as if two huge men were necessary to keep me in line. The square was no longer empty, and the air throbbed with anticipation, the glee even thicker than the humidity during the peak of summer. Saffron stood front and center, wrapped in her cloak as usual, the thick fabric protecting her from the hot sun pounding down on the city. Lysander and Bastian wore robes as well, each of them in their chairs, and across their laps they had identical electroprods ready and waiting in case they were needed.

I searched the stage for Bodhi, but he was nowhere in sight. Mira was present though, standing in line with the other housemaids, her face streaked in tears. Then there was Asa. He was in the last line of Fortis guards, and he stared at me openly as I was dragged by him, his brown eyes giving off an emotion that both confused me and made my steps clumsy.

"Bring her here," Saffron ordered, pointing her electroprod at the ground by her side.

The men pulled me to the front of the stage, and once there I was pushed to my knees, right next to Saffron. I had expected to be bound, but I found my hands free. Was it a test? A message? If I obeyed Saffron she would be merciful, but if I moved I would be punished more severely. If that was her plan, she would be disappointed. It was impossible to care about what they were going to do to me, not with everything else going on, and I had no intention of being still. Bodhi was my husband, and if I had to die trying, I would have my goodbye.

When Greer and the other guard had taken their places in line, the doors at the back of the stage once again opened. I twisted my body so I could get a better look, and seconds later Bodhi was pulled from the building, squinting from the bright light. He was struggling, but his arms were behind his back and two large men flanked him. It would be no use. He was no match for the Fortis, and even if he did somehow manage to get away, there were more than a dozen other men and women lined up on the stage at his back and even more throughout the square. Bodhi had no chance. None of us did.

He was brought to the center of the stage and pushed down on his knees just as I had been. Our positions were too far apart to allow us to touch, but close enough that it made my stomach lurch. Saffron had been serious about me having a front row seat.

"This Outlier is accused of attempted murder," she began, her voice ringing through the square and bringing a stop to all conversation. "He not only broke into my home, but he attacked my son." She waved her electroprod in Lysander's direction. "For the crime of attempted murder, he will be put to death right here, right now. By beheading."

The world swayed and I had to put my hands on the ground to stop from falling over. Mira's sobs were the only thing I could hear. I knew there had to be more noises, whispers from the crowd or the wind, but I could hear none of them. I looked toward my husband as I tried to wrap my brain around what was about to happen, and I found him watching me. He had one tear on his cheek. One single tear that had escaped from his right eye and was now making a trail down his face.

Movement at his back caught my eye and I shifted my gaze. A man was walking forward, a sword in his hand. The sun glinted off the blade and I squinted, but still it was impossible to make sense of the scene in front of me. Sobs made me look back, past the man. Mira was crying harder than ever. So hard that her shoulders shook.

Crying for me.

Crying for Bodhi.

Because he was about to be killed.

Everything seemed to hit me at once. The emotionless way Saffron had announced my husband's death, the gleam in Lysander's eyes, the cool way the guard looked at Bodhi as he carried the sword forward. It slammed into me, forcing the air out of my lungs and nearly knocking me on my ass. Bodhi was about to die.

"No," I mumbled, and then I started crawling. "No."

The tears came out like a faucet had been turned on behind my eyes. Bodhi was shaking his head, telling me to stay back. I was unable to stop. I crawled faster, and then scrambled to my feet. Behind me Saffron was shouting for me to get back in position, still I refused to stop, refused to even look at her. All I could do was run to my husband and pray that this was a nightmare.

I dropped to the ground in front of Bodhi and threw my arms around him. I kissed his cheeks as I sobbed and hugged him. His arms did not go around me back, and when I realized he still had his hands tied, I tried to undo the knot. I just wanted his arms around me one more time. I wanted to feel safe for one final moment, because I knew that after today I would never feel that way again. Not if Bodhi was gone. Not if I were left alone.

"I love you," I said, still trying to undo the knot. Hands grabbed me and pulled me away from him, and I screamed out, "I love you!"

"I love you, Indra," Bodhi called as I was dragged away. "I am sorry. I am so sorry."

I clawed at the ground, trying to get to him. My nails broke and my fingers began to bleed, but I felt none of it. I felt nothing but the shattering of my heart, and I was certain that it would crush me.

When I was far enough away from Bodhi, the guard who had grabbed me pushed me onto my stomach. A knee was pressed against my spine, reminding me of the day Ronan had lost his hand, and then a voice whispered in my ear, "Be still, Indra, or you'll die too. Your husband wouldn't want that."

I kept my eyes forward, but Asa's words somehow reached me when nothing else had and I stopped fighting. Bodhi was back in position. On his knees, facing forward with his hands tied behind his back, and the man with the sword was behind him. Time seemed to freeze as my husband looked my way one last time. The blue eyes I had known for as long as I could remember held mine, and a million memories went through my head. Us as children, playing in the forest, Bodhi chasing me as I laughed, always just a little bit faster than him. Later out in the woods before my father died, knowing that he loved me. Our wedding day, kneeling side by side as his father carved the passage markings onto our foreheads. Our wedding night, the cave, standing looking at the ruins, Bodhi holding me, Bodhi kissing me, Bodhi promising to love me forever. Bodhi telling me that he would never leave me.

He blinked and looked away, and then the blade was cutting through the air, the metal seeming to glow in the rays of the sun. Then, in the blink of an eye, Bodhi was gone. Forever.

Asa's knee left my back, but I stayed where I was. I was unable to move. Around me the world shifted. People moved and Bodhi's body was carried away, to where I had no clue.

Still I stayed on the ground. Tears fell from my eyes. The sobs from earlier had melted away and in their place a feeling of nothingness had settled over me. It was unlike anything I had ever experienced before. I felt dead.

Even when strong hands pulled me up I felt nothing. They dragged me forward, right through the puddle of blood that had pooled on the platform, and back to the center of the stage where I was forced down once again. Floggings had become so commonplace that I almost felt as if I had been here before, on my stomach in front of hundreds of people, my cheek pressed against the cold ground. Only I had not, and even in my numb state I knew that the shattering of my world had only begun. Bodhi's death was just the beginning, and the Sovereign would never let me leave here today until they had dominated me in every way possible.

My hair was pushed aside and someone slid the blade of a knife down the back of my dress, cutting the fabric away and exposing the flawless skin beneath. Had I not fought they would have gone easier on me. It was too late to do anything else, and even if I could redo it, I would have done nothing different.

In the midst of this crisis, I had forgotten all about my injuries from the day before. When they tied my hands together the sensitive skin on my wrists cried out, reminding me of what had already been done to my body. How much more could I go through and still live? I already felt half dead, maybe more than half, and now they were going to whip me.

"Just kill me," I found myself whispering.

Saffron came to stand at my side, looking down at me

from under her hood with cool eyes. "This will teach you a much greater lesson."

She turned away and nodded, and then she was gone and the same man who had removed my husband's head from his body took her place. The whip in his hand was the same one I had seen dozens of times over the last few months, and I knew what was coming. I closed my eyes and waited for the pain.

The first strike sent a rush of agony across my back and caused my whole body to jerk. I screamed, and before the sound had a chance to fade away, the whip struck my back a second time. Another cry came out of my mouth. The third strike was the same, but after that I was sobbing too hard to get more than whimpers out.

Saffron had not told me how many lashes I would receive, and I lost count after five, but it seemed to go on forever. It was pain on top of pain, and there seemed to be no break between lashes. Over and over again the man brought the whip down until the world around me grew dark, and when that happened, I was finally given the relief I had been craving since the moment Bodhi was caught.

I WAS ON THE GROUND WHEN I REGAINED consciousness, still lying on my stomach. It was hard under my body, but cool against my skin, and compared to the heat that licked at my back, it was almost comforting. It was as if I could feel every single place the whip had lashed against my skin, all of the cuts and welts throbbing at once.

"Indra." Mira knelt at my side, and when my eyes focused, I realized I was still on the stage.

I looked toward the square to find that it had begun to clear out. A few people still hung around, staring at me as if I were on display, but most were leaving. I turned my head, groaning when the muscles in my back flexed, making my whole body scream out in pain. The chairs Saffron and her family had been sitting in were empty, and beyond that the housemaids had left as well. There were still a few Fortis guards milling around though, and I wondered what they were waiting for. Did they have orders to take me back to the dark cell? To whip me again when I woke? Did some other horror await me now that I had finally regained consciousness?

"The doctor is coming," Mira said, drawing my gaze back to her. "Saffron said to wait for him. Once he has a chance to look at you, we can leave."

I nodded and more pain licked at my back, making me cry out.

"Try not to move," Mira whispered. She reached out like she was going to touch me, but her hands stayed hovered above my body.

I wanted to point out that we had an hour walk ahead of us. Right now I was unable to muster even enough strength to get the words out, let alone think about the long trek through the borderland. Not when I had no idea how I would get through it.

Mira stood and I watched from my place on the ground as she walked across the podium. She stopped in front of Asa, and even through the painful haze clouding my brain I was shocked when she met his gaze. They spoke for only a moment, much too far away for me to catch even a single word, and then Asa left and Mira headed back to me.

Before I could ask her anything the same doctor who had examined Ronan appeared. He was an older man with frizzy white hair and a scowl that told me he thought examining Outliers was beneath him, but he did his job and looked me over.

"It will heal fine," he said.

His fingers brushed my back and my body jerked. I let out a hiss of pain as I squeezed my eyes shut. The doctor said something else but I had no idea what it was. Mira was there though, she would tell me what I needed to know.

When I opened my eyes, my gaze focused on a dark spot in front of me. It was small, no bigger than the tip of my thumb, and at first I was unable to figure out what it was. Instinctively, though, I knew it was important. I knew it had something to do with what had happened here today.

Then my brain focused on the fact that it was blood and it all came back. It was Bodhi's blood. He had died here today, killed by the Sovereign. Beheaded and tossed aside like he was nothing. The tears that filled my eyes blurred out the spot, but they did nothing to erase what I had witnessed here today. Nothing ever would.

"Indra." Mira pressed something against my lips. "Drink this. It will dull the pain so we can get home."

I obeyed, sucking the sweet liquid down as I thought about the day not that long ago when I had done the same thing for Ronan.

We did not wait for the drug to take effect, and when Mira helped me to my feet it was the most excruciating experience I had ever been through—with the exception of watching my husband die. I sank my teeth into my bottom lip, trying to bite back the gasps of pain, but it was no use. I could do nothing without causing myself more suffering. Not stand, not walk, not even breathe. Every move hurt, and I knew that the agony would remain long after my physical injuries had healed.

I barely remembered getting through the city, but before I knew it we were in front of the gate. Mira stayed with me every step of the way, just as she had yesterday, only today I felt certain that even with her help I would be unable to make it home.

"Mira." We were only a few steps out of the city, but already I felt as if I were going to collapse. "I cannot go on."

She wrapped her arm more firmly around me and I bit back a cry of pain. "You just have a little further to go. Hold on."

She had said the same thing yesterday, only then I had been able to cling to the lie and pretend it was true. Today, it was impossible. Not with the Fortis village stretching out in front of us for what seemed like forever. Not with our enemies lining up to watch my continued destruction.

"No." I stopped walking and tried to sit down. "I cannot."

Mira pulled me forward, refusing to allow me to sink down the way I wanted to. She was sobbing again, her body shaking as she pulled on me. "Walk, Indra. Now. You cannot give up." Her words were nearly drowned out by her sobs.

"Do not leave me. Promise that you will never leave me."

The words rang through my head, reminding me of last night in my hut, lying next to Bodhi. I had said almost the same thing to him, but he had broken the promise and left me, and now I was in pieces. Not just physically, either. My back was shredded, I knew that without being able to see it, but so were my insides. Bodhi had left me, and in the process I had been ripped apart.

I refused to do that to my friend. Refused to put my sister and mother through that if I could prevent it.

"I will never leave you, Mira." I forced my legs to move. "I promise."

By some miracle we made it through the village, and then passed into the boundary lands. The edges of my vision were dark, as if the fingers of death were trying to pull me to the underworld, but I was still able to make out Asa in the distance. He stood beside the rock that concealed our weapons, and at his side was a horse. The sight of him brought me to my knees.

"Indra," he gasped out my name as he rushed to kneel in front of me.

His hands stopped just short of touching me. I was unsure if it was because of what had happened earlier in the mudroom, or because he was afraid of hurting me.

"Thank you," Mira gasped from above me.

Asa looked up at her and then back at me. "This is my fault. I wasn't there to protect you yesterday and I'll never forgive myself for it, but I will make sure you get home." He held his hand out. "Let me help you."

I took his hand just as Mira grabbed my arm, and between the two of them I was able to get to my feet. Getting on the horse was another story. Asa was tall, which helped, but every move I made was agony and there was no way to get myself seated on the animal without excruciating pain. By the time I had managed it, with a lot of help from both Asa and Mira, my face was streaked in tears.

My head was swimming, and I felt certain that if I had to remain sitting up I would pass out, so I leaned forward and rested my head against the horse's mane, holding onto his neck so I did not fall off. Mira climbed on behind me and gingerly held onto my waist so she would know if I started to lose my balance while Asa took his place at the front of the horse. He urged the animal to walk, and each step was torturous. Not just because of the pain though, but also because it brought me closer to home. I wanted to be back in my village, back with my mother and Anja, but I also knew that once we arrived I would have a long road of healing ahead of me. Both physically and emotionally.

I stayed that way for most of the ride, clinging to consciousness as desperately as I was clinging to the horse as pain pulsed across my back with every move the animal made. Once or twice the darkness threatened to win, but each time I managed to hold on. How, I had no idea.

Someone must have spotted us from the distance, because before we had even reached the edge of the village people were rushing out to greet us. I was in too much pain to focus, but I did register it when Mira slid off the horse.

Around me people were talking, but concentrating on their words was impossible. Some of the voices sounded familiar, including Asa's. How Mira was going to explain his presence was a mystery I could not focus on. Not when I was so close to falling into an abyss of blackness.

"Indra."

He was at my side, his hands on me, somehow helping me off the horse while avoiding the parts of my body that ached the most. Then he was helping me walk, and when the darkness finally closed in to claim me, I felt him lift me into his arms.

TWENTY-ONE

WHEN I WOKE, I FOUND MYSELF ON MY stomach once again. Only now I was in a bed. Not the one I had shared with Bodhi, but the one that I had at one time shared with my sister.

Anja was asleep at my side, curled up in a ball on the very edge, but the rest of the bed was empty. I shifted, trying to find my mother, and immediately regretted it when pain pulsed through me.

"Shhh." There was movement, followed by footsteps, and then she was at my side, brushing the hair off my forehead. "Do not move."

"How long have I been asleep?"

"Many hours," she said. "But not long enough." Her hand left my forehead and a second later she had a vial in front of my lips, the same one the doctor in the city had given Mira. "Drink, and then go back to sleep."

I did as I was told, knowing that it would help ease my discomfort, but also knowing that sleep would evade me until I had answers to my questions.

"What happened?" I asked.

"You do not remember?" My mother settled on the bed next to me, her hand once again on my head.

"I mean after I passed out. Asa was here. What happened to him?"

"The Fortis man who helped you," my mother said, but it was not a question. "He brought you to our hut and helped me get you settled. He refused to leave until he knew you were okay. Adina came and checked your wounds. We undressed you and the Fortis man turned away, but he still refused to leave. The healer washed your back and applied leaves, and then she left us, but still he stayed."

"Is he gone now?" I asked.

"He left some time ago, after he was sure you were only sleeping and not dying." My mother's hand stopped moving, and when I looked up, I found her studying my face. "This man is in love with you."

"He has been helping us," I said, not wanting to acknowledge Asa's feelings out loud to my mother but refusing to lie to her. "He is better than the others."

"I can see that, but Indra, you are a married woman."

"I was," I whispered, and a tear escaped from the corner of my eye. "It was not like that for me. I loved Bodhi. I still love him. But inside the city, Asa looked out for me. That is it."

Her hand started moving over my head once more, and it was soothing. Like I was a child again. "I am sorry about Bodhi."

I closed my eyes, trying to hold the tears in. They spilled over anyway. It was impossible to wipe them away without putting myself in pain, so I let them flow from my eyes and down my cheeks.

"He promised that he would stay away from the city."

"Sometimes we do things because we feel like we do not have a choice. Maybe this was one of those things for Bodhi."

Her words reminded me of what Asa had said in the mudroom and I murmured, "Maybe he could not have lived with himself if he had done nothing."

"Maybe," she said.

She went silent, but her hand kept moving, kept running down my head the way it had hundreds of times in my life. When I was sick or sad, when I was hurt. When we lost my father. It was so comforting that I felt myself start to drift off, felt the darkness begin to pull me down and the pain start to recede.

"I know your pain, my daughter. I have been there." My body jerked at the sound of my mother's voice, but if she noticed she made no indication. Instead she continued talking. "I was not like you. I did not run from love. When your father asked for my heart, I gave it to him freely. We were young. So much younger than you and Bodhi, but we loved one another deeply. Just as you loved your husband.

"There was so much heartbreak for us, so much disappointment and loss, but we weathered it all together and we were happy. And then we got you, and then Anja, and it felt as if God was trying to make up for everything He had taken from us. My heart was full, as was my life, and I believed that nothing would ever change that."

A drop of moisture landed on my cheek, but it took a moment in my drugged haze to realize it was a tear. My mother was crying. I wanted to open my eyes, to look up and see her face. My eyes refused to obey, and so they stayed closed while my mother ran her hand down my head over and over again.

"I never told you what really happened. It was too hard. Maybe it was wrong. Maybe I should have given you more credit, but you were young and I was afraid the truth would be too much for you. Afraid that it would fill your life with fear or rage.

"Your father was out hunting, that much you know, but he was not attacked by a forest cat. It was not an animal at all, but a man. Or a group of them. The Fortis hunters must have taken him by surprise because he was always careful. He always watched his back. When he failed to come home that night, I knew. I knew what had happened. It was not until the next afternoon that they found his body."

She paused and let out a deep breath and I desperately tried to force my eyes to open, but they remained closed. "For a short time after that I was so sad and angry and broken that I wanted to die. I had you girls to take care of, and it pulled me out of the dark pit I found myself in. It was difficult, but necessary. I know you will have hard times my daughter, but you must do everything you can to find a purpose in this life. One that will keep you from falling into the pit of despair left in the wake of your husband's death."

She went on, her words becoming more and more fuzzy as the moments passed until they were nothing but murmurs on the wind. And then the blackness pulled me in, wrapping me in its comforting embrace.

I SPENT MY DAYS LYING ON MY STOMACH. ADINA kept watch over my wounds while my mother and sister took care of my other needs. Once we ran out of the medicine from Sovereign City, I found sleep nearly impossible. I woke screaming from dreams where I had to watch my husband get beheaded over and over again, where Lysander forced me down, right on top of Bodhi's body. Where grizzards pecked at me while Fortis guards watched with glee in their eyes. It was a never-ending nightmare, but not nearly as torturous as the reality I woke to. The one where Bodhi was gone for good.

When I was finally allowed to get up and move around a little, I found it nearly impossible. Between my lack of rest and my injuries, I had no energy. Just walking around the hut wore me out, but I was relieved to be out of bed. More than that, I wanted to get my stamina back up. Lying in the hut all day meant I had nothing to do but think, and since that moment I woke up in my hut to find Bodhi gone, he had been the only thing on my mind.

I thought about all the wasted years I had spent running from my feelings. All the time I could have been with him but had instead refused to allow myself to give in. Now, looking back on it all, I had no idea why I had done it. Why had I resisted something I had so obviously wanted? Why had I refused to allow Bodhi to love me when that was all he had ever wanted to do? I had no answers, which made it so much worse, and all I wanted was a distraction from the constant pain of knowing that I had lost so much.

My job in the city was out of the question. Going back was impossible. Even if I was allowed to return to my position, which I was uncertain of, I would never again be able to look Saffron and Lysander in the eye. I also knew that I had to find a new way to provide for my family. The rations and medicine the Sovereign used to provide us with would be missed, and before long we would all suffer from the loss of it. My mother most of all. There had to be something I could do.

I thought about all those hours Bodhi and I had spent together in the woods and how I had felt after killing my first forest cat, and it felt like the answer I needed. The solution to what I would do without my job, as well as how to distract myself from thoughts of my dead husband.

Only, I was not ready to move on. Not yet. Even if my body had been healed enough to allow me to go out and hunt, my soul was not. I had to say my final goodbyes to Bodhi.

The Winta had very specific rituals for dealing with death. Things that ensured our departed would be welcomed into the afterlife following their passing. The bodies of our dead were supposed to be burned, but since the Sovereign had held onto Bodhi's body, it was a ceremony we were unable to perform. I could only pray that he would still be able to rest in peace, because the idea of Bodhi not being admitted into the afterlife was more painful than the lashes I had received.

Even without the ceremony there were things that needed to be done. Things that I had been too injured to participate in before. Now that I was up and moving around, I was anxious to get them taken care of. Not just so I could move on, but so I could say my final goodbyes to my husband.

Everyone gathered for the ceremony, just as they had on the night that Bodhi and I were married. Old and young, men and women, they all congregated in the center of the village where the large fire was already burning. I sat on the ground at the front of the group, my back facing the fire and feeling its heat more than ever, while Bodhi's family knelt at my side. My mother came to kneel in front of me, aided by my sister, who also held the bowl of dye while our mother wielded the tebori. She tapped it against my skin, under the lines that moved up my cheekbones. There she drew another half circle, looping it up so it captured the first one. The one that represented my father. She did this first on the right cheek, and then on the left, drawing blood from my skin and tears from my eyes that had nothing to do with the pain. When she was finished, she dipped her fingers in the bowl and rubbed the dye into the cuts just as Bodhi's father had done on my wedding day, only these passage markings failed to make me feel complete the way those had. These marked me as a widow. As someone who had lost more than they should have at such a young age.

When she was finished, my mother took a clean cloth and washed my face. First the blood and dye from my skin, and then the tears from my eyes.

"Your husband will be with you always," she said.

"May your travels to the afterlife be swift," I whispered, reciting our traditional prayer for the dead to myself. Even though we had no body to burn, Bodhi still deserved a proper send off. "And may the transgressions you have committed on earth not prevent you from resting in peace eternal."

Then I closed my eyes, focusing on the pain in my cheeks as I thought about Bodhi, and I told myself that her words were true. He was gone, but he would always be a part of me. Not just in the passage markings, but in my heart, in the village, and the people living here. In the forest we had spent so much time together in, in the caves, and the bow he had lovingly taught me to use. He had died, but Bodhi would always be with me because he had changed who I was. Both with his life, and with his death.

MIRA BROUGHT NEWS OF THE CITY BACK TO ME, BUT we never talked about me returning to my job. It was a subject we both knew would be pointless to discuss. After everything that had happened, I was unable to stomach the thought of walking through that gate ever again.

"Asa asks after you," she said as I walked gingerly through the forest at her side.

"He still watches over you?" I asked her.

"More than ever."

"He is a good man," I said. "I never thought I would be able to say that about a Fortis, but it is true. Asa is a good man."

"He is," my friend agreed.

Every day after Mira returned from work, she walked with me into the woods, and each day I was able to go a little further. Three weeks had passed since Bodhi's death, and I was healing and getting stronger, but still not sleeping any better, which was affecting my ability to do much. I needed rest, only the nights brought too much horror. They brought me dreams of the Fortis and the square where my life had changed, of grizzards tearing my husband apart while Saffron watched.

It had gotten so bad that if not for how much Asa had done for me, I doubted I would want to hear anyone talk about Sovereign City ever again. Still, every time Mira mentioned the man who had saved me, I felt something in my heart that made me believe I might actually be able to heal with time. It felt as if all the months of seeing how wonderful Asa could be had carved out a place for him, a place that remained uninjured—the only part of my heart that was still whole—and had instead given me faith in people. In the existence of goodness.

My feelings for Asa were different than the ones he had for me. I had no reason to believe they ever could be—if I ever saw him again, which I doubted—but he had done what he promised and protected me inside the walls, and for that he would always have a place in my heart.

If anything good came out of my injury, it was the extra time I was able to spend with my mother. She was growing weaker by the day, something that was magnified by the loss of the medicine I had been bringing her from the city. Just getting out of bed wore her out, and it seemed as if she had begun to wither away before my very eyes. I worried that she was in pain, only whenever I asked, she insisted that she was fine.

I tried to take on the majority of her care even though I was still healing. My sister's eyes had lost some of their light with Bodhi's death, and it had even affected her relationship with Jax. I knew that it had taken almost as much of a toll on her as it had on me. Bodhi's death, my whipping, and now our mother's rapidly declining health. My sister was young still, and even though I knew she was strong, I did not want her to have to be. Not when I could carry the load.

Nearly a month went by before Xandra visited me. I had not seen her since returning to the village, but it was something I had been thankful for. I remembered the part she had played in Bodhi's death, and even though my husband had made his own choices, I was unable to think about Xandra without putting the majority of the blame on her shoulders. She must have known what would happen when she chose to lead him into the city, yet she had done it anyway. It was something I was unable to think about without a great amount of hate burning inside me.

I was in the middle of eating lunch when Xandra stopped by. My mother was with me, and since she was much too weak to excuse herself, she waved for me to go to the other side of the hut to talk. I obeyed even though I was certain that I had nothing to say to Xandra. At that moment, I was positive that I would not have been able to shed even a single tear if someone told me the woman had been ripped apart by grizzards inside the city.

Xandra was a good ten years older than me, but still unmarried, which was a rare occurrence in our village. The Winta believed that a woman needed a man to take care of her, and yet Xandra had chosen to remain in her mother's hut. She was not an unattractive woman. In fact, she had what I considered to be striking features, with high cheekbones and full lips. Even more, she was tall and sturdy for an Outlier, with shoulders that were much broader than the average woman, and her light brown skin was both smooth and had a healthy glow to it. She kept her dark hair short, not shaved like Anja and my mother did, and it suited her features.

"I have been wanting to talk to you," she began.

On the other side of the hut, my mother had turned so she was on her side, her back to us, but I knew she was listening.

"You should have talked to me earlier," I said. "Before you led Bodhi into the city."

Xandra's brown eyes moved to the ground. "I am sorry for my part, Indra. When he came to me that morning, I told him I would not take him there. I told him that he would die. That he would be leaving you alone. But he refused to let up. He followed me through the borderland, and when we got closer to the city, I knew that I had to make a choice. If I led him into the city through the tunnel he had a chance, but if I kept going and he followed me to the gate, there would be nothing I could do to save him. He would have died in the Fortis village, before he even made it inside. I did what I thought best, and even though I know it will not comfort you to hear it, I believe that it was the only thing I could have done." She ventured a look up, keeping her head bowed. "I prayed that he would make it safely. I hope you can remember that when you look at me, and that one day you will be able to forgive me for the part I played in this."

"You led my husband to his death." My voice cracked and I knew that soon I would be crying, but I found it impossible to keep the tears in.

Bodhi was dead because of what Xandra had done. She had killed him, and now she was standing in front of me, asking me to forgive her. It was impossible. Just as I would never be able to look at Xandra without thinking about the sword cutting my husband's head off, or the pain of the whip on my back.

She stayed where she was, but the sobs had clogged my throat too much to say anything else, so I turned my back on her.

Only a moment passed before the beat of her footsteps told me that she was leaving, and when the door shut behind her, I allowed my sobs to break free. Holding them back would have been impossible, anyway.

On the other side of the hut, my mother shifted and I turned to find her watching me.

"Your anger is misdirected, Indra."

I swiped my hand across my face. "It is not. Xandra led Bodhi into the city even though she knew he would die. How can I *forgive* her for that? Could you?"

My mother pushed herself up with great effort, and even though I was still hurting and sad, I hurried to her side.

"I am okay." She waved me off when I reached for her, and her brown eyes focused on me. "Xandra is not who you are angry at. It is Bodhi. He is the one who broke his word. He is the one who went into the city. I know that being mad at him feels wrong, but do not confuse your feelings, Indra. You and I both know he alone is responsible for his actions."

I started to shake my head, but it was no use. She was right. The Sovereign had caused this and they had used the Fortis to kill my husband, but he had made his own choices. He was the one who decided he had to go into the city. He was the one who had put Xandra in an impossible situation.

I swallowed and met my mother's gaze. "I am so angry at him for leaving me. So hurt."

"It is normal." She took my hand in hers and gave it a squeeze. "You will heal over time, and as you do you will learn how to forgive him. You may even find that you will come to understand why he chose to do something so risky."

"What do I do until then?" I pressed my free hand against my chest. "How do I stop the pain whenever I think about him?"

"You cannot. You just need to find something else to live for. Something that means as much to you as Bodhi did."

It was impossible to imagine anything or anyone in the world that would ever mean as much to me as my husband, but I nodded anyway.

TWENTY-TWO

T HE DAY FINALLY CAME WHEN I WAS STRONG enough to go out into the woods to hunt. For weeks I had been waiting for this moment, for the freedom and distractions the forest would bring, and lying in my hut with nothing to do, it had sounded like the ideal solution. Only, now that the opportunity was in front of me, I suddenly found that I was less excited than I had been before. Something was holding me back.

Summer had not yet come to an end and the sun still beat down on the wilds as if wanting to set them on fire, only it was not the heat that made me hesitate. I found the vast expanse of the wilds scary. Bodhi and I had gone out into the woods together to shoot dozens of times, but I had never been out there on my own before, and I was suddenly unsure if I could do it.

Standing at the edge of the village with a sheath of arrows on my back and a bow in my hand, it hit me just how much I had really lost. Not only had my partner in life been stolen from me, but also my hunting partner and protector, and the man who had vowed to take care of me for the rest of my life. I was alone again, and as a Winta woman, that was a very big thing.

I was an Outlier, not Sovereign, and in the wilds women did not rule, especially not women from my tribe. My whole life I had been taught that I needed a man to take care of me; that I was too weak to do it on my own, and even the help and encouragement my husband had given me when he was alive was unable to completely erase the teachings I had grown up with.

Still, there was a part of me that knew I *needed* this. Not just for me, but for my family as well. My job in the city was gone, taking with it the extra provisions we had always depended on, and it was up to me to do something to provide for my family. If I did nothing they would suffer, and that was something I could not stomach even thinking about.

It was the prospect of my mother and sister starving that finally forced me into the woods. Still, I was hesitant. At first I stayed close to the village, always sure that the huts were within my sight. I was far enough away that I felt wrapped in the surrounding wilderness. It was quiet and welcome, peaceful even, and it gave me courage to go further.

So I did. I moved away from the village, deeper into the wilds in search of game just as I had done with Bodhi dozens of times before. I knew that the greenery of the forest would make it difficult to track the animals, but I was certain that if I tried hard enough I would be able to get something. I had to. My family needed it.

My first day out, however, I returned to the village with no more than I had left with. There had been a couple moments when I had thought I might get a kill, but I was out of practice and still sore at times, and my arrow missed every time. Still, being in the woods was even more reinvigorating than I had anticipated. It had made me feel closer to Bodhi, like he was in the forest with me, watching over me the entire time. It eased my tired mind so much that when I lay down that night, I drifted off immediately, and for the first time since Bodhi's death, I did not dream.

The next day I returned to the woods without hesitation, and even though I still went home with no game, my aim was improving. Day three came and I repeated the process, going deep into the woods in search of game, only this time I actually managed to take out one of the small rodents that were common in the forest. The surge of pride that shot through me when I collected the animal was the same one I had felt the first time I killed a forest cat, only there was something else too. I felt as if I had found my place in the village, or maybe even a purpose in life, and it gave me a peace I had not felt since before Ronan's punishment.

My life continued on this way. I went out into the forest in the morning, hunting for game while gathering any nuts, berries, or mushrooms I came upon. Some days I wandered far from the village, as far as the cliff behind the cave Bodhi and I had visited so many times, while other days I kept closer to home. Any game I got was brought back to the village and split between my family and Ronan's, the leftovers going to the Head to distribute among other needy families. While none of the men were happy that I had taken to hunting in the woods alone, no one tried to stop me. And they were not foolish enough to refuse the meat I brought in.

My mother seemed to improve a little, as if my lifted spirits were medicine, and even Anja looked more at peace and once again began spending time with Jax. Our wounds were still healing and we still missed Bodhi's presence, but more than ever before I felt as if his spirit was watching over me. During the day, as I traveled the wilds in search of food, I felt him with me. In the hut at night, eating the food I had brought in thanks to his instruction, it seemed as if he was constantly at my side.

It still took quite a bit of time before I was able to be around Bodhi's family, something I felt his disapproval over. His father, mother, and brothers were suffering over his loss just as much as I was, but being with them had at first hurt too much. Ilian was approaching his fifteenth year, and his resemblance to his older brother was so stark that it nearly took my breath away. I could see Bodhi in every tilt of Ilian's lips, in the way he helped his younger brother do things around the hut, in how much he cared for his mother and father. At first when I had been healed enough to move around I had gone to see them a few times, only to find that being in their presence had been too painful. But, thanks to my time in the forest, I found that this was another part of myself that healed.

Nearly six weeks had passed since Bodhi's death when I happened upon Ilian as I was returning from the forest. The urge to duck away before he could see me hit, but a whisper in my ear that could only have been the spirit of my husband urged me to call out to him. When I did, the boy's face lit up, and I found that even though the smile he gave me was the same as Bodhi's, it did not sting, but instead filled me with warmth. That was when it hit me that Bodhi was here as well, in his family and in the village. And it filled me with peace.

Weeks passed and my heart and soul healed a little more each day. Not as thoroughly as my back had, but enough that I no longer felt like a broken plate that had been glued together. I hunted, spent time with my family, and allowed myself to grieve. It was all I could do, but it was beginning to be enough.

I had been going out into the forest for nearly two months when I decided to head further east, toward the river. It was a direction Bodhi had never taken me, and even though I knew why and the dangers that accompanied being so close to Fortis territory, I found myself moving in that direction without reason or thought. But I had not even reached the valley the river ran through when the beat of horse hooves broke through the silence of the forest.

The one and only time Bodhi and I had come across a Fortis hunter in the woods, we had hidden, and at that moment, alone and shaking, it was all I could think to do. I crouched down behind a bush, careful to stay out of sight. A blink later they were in front of me, seemingly coming from out of nowhere as they materialized from the thick foliage the wilds offered. Fortis hunters.

There were two of them, both on horseback and both loaded down with weapons and the spoils of their long day in the wilds. The one man had three of the small rodents that were so plentiful in our part of the woods, as well as a rawlin, its feathers bright red against the black horse, while the second had a large forest cat draped over the back of his horse. It was a lot of food, more than I would probably be able to get in a week, and the sight of it sent my mind whirling.

It was unfair how the Fortis always had so much when we were given so little. They had the help of the Sovereign, who grew fruits and vegetables in their climate controlled buildings, while we had to scrounge to survive. No wonder they were big and strong while we wasted away.

When I notched my arrow though, I was not thinking about the food and how much it would mean for my village. I was thinking about Mira helping me from the city, after Bodhi's death and my flogging. That was the last time I had seen any of the Fortis, and seeing them now, remembering the man who had so callously cut Bodhi's head off and then whipped me until I was certain I would be joining my husband, filled me with rage. I did not even pause to consider what I was doing or why I was doing it, or even what the consequences might be, I simply pulled the string on my bow back and stood.

The second I released the arrow I regretted it, but by then it was too late. It flew through the air, finding a home in the head of the man closest to me. He went down before his friend had a chance to even look around, his body hitting the forest floor with a thud I knew I would never forget. By the time the second man had turned his head in my direction, I already had another arrow notched, and his eyes met mine only a beat before the point sank into his throat.

The horse startled, throwing the injured man from its back. It trotted around in a circle but did not take off, and neither did the second horse. I also stayed where I was. My head was screaming for me to run, but I was frozen. All I could do was stare at the two men I had just shot.

That's when it occurred to me that these two men might not be the only hunters in the woods. I notched another arrow as I looked around, holding my breath and straining my ears for any sound that might indicate there were others, but the woods were silent except for the sounds of nature. Leaves rustling above my head, the scratch of small feet scurrying through the forest, and the whoosh of hot wind pushing its way through the trees. Nothing else.

When I was certain no one else was coming, I darted over to the men. The first one was already dead, and the lifeless blue eyes that stared up at me gave me pause as the reality of what I had done hit me. I had killed a man. Taken a life. The Winta were not great warriors like the Huni, but we did hunt and eat animals. But even then, the taking of a life was not something we did thoughtlessly. We only killed what we needed, and we used every part of the animal. We did not hunt for sport the way the Mountari and Huni did, and we never killed other people.

Guilt rushed through me. Guilt over the life I had taken, over how little I had thought about it before I had released my arrow.

Then the face of the dead man morphed, and suddenly the person in front of me was the same man who had wielded the sword that took my husband's life. Then it was Greer's face, and then Thorin's. It changed again and again, and each time I saw the face of a man or woman who had tortured and abused my people, the guilt became less intense. In no time every ounce of remorse I felt at taking his life had been sucked away and replaced by satisfaction. Satisfaction that he would never be able to hurt anyone again, that there was one less Fortis man who could rape and beat and plunder my people.

I turned to the second man and found him choking on his own blood. He was also staring up at me, but his expression seemed more surprised by the sight of me than scared at the prospect of dying. This time there was no guilt, and there was also no hesitation. Even though I knew he would very soon be joining his friend, I pulled out my knife and plunged it into the man's head anyway, and he finally went still.

Now I had not just taken one life, but two. I stood over the bodies, staring down at their empty expressions as I waited for the remorse to come, knowing that it should and that it would be a legitimate feeling if it did. I had shot these men out of revenge, an act that I was certain would follow me into the afterlife. Still, staring at their lifeless bodies, I could feel nothing but satisfaction. There was no guilt inside me. Not after everything that had happened.

I was, however, concerned that someone would find the evidence of what I had done and come to my village to get their own revenge. The first thing I needed to do was cover up the fact that an Outlier was responsible for the deaths. I pulled my arrows from the men's bodies, but I took nothing else, not wanting it to look as if they had been robbed. Hopefully, the animals in the forest would get to the men before anyone found their bodies, and it would help cover my tracks further. Once that happened, it would be impossible to tell that an arrow had ended their lives.

Even though I still felt no remorse for what I had done, I found myself kneeling next to the bodies anyway. I was uncertain whether or not the Fortis believed in a god or the afterlife, but as a member of the Winta tribe, I felt compelled to do something for these men as their spirits left their earthly shells. Only the traditional Winta prayer felt wrong. These men did not deserve swift travels to the afterlife. They did not deserve to be anywhere near my husband or the other souls who had been ripped from this world at their hands.

My mind spun, and on instinct I lowered my head and instead whispered the simple prayer reserved for animals, and the moment the words left my lips, I knew it had been the right choice. "May your death provide life to our people and sustain us through hard times."

Once that was done, I freed the smaller game from the first man's horse and smacked the animal on the rump, sending him charging into the woods. If he was found they would probably assume that a forest cat had hurt his rider, or possibly even a flock of rawlin. No one in the Fortis village would ever consider that an Outlier was responsible for the death. At least not without evidence.

The second horse carried the cat, so I pulled myself up on its back and directed it to turn around. The cat was much too big for me to carry very far, so my plan was to ride the horse as close to the village as I could before unloading it and sending it after its friend. I still felt no remorse for what I had done, but the Winta would never look kindly on the fact that I had taken human life. Even humans so unworthy of the air they breathed.

Everything went exactly as planned. I stopped the horse just out of sight of our village and pulled the carcass down before sending the horse on his way, and then I dragged the animals through the trees. The second someone in the village spotted me, I had help. Everyone assumed I had killed the animals myself; there was no other explanation that made sense. No one had a clue where the game had actually come from.

I expected the guilt that had evaded me in the forest to come that night when I lay down to sleep, but still it did not come. Instead, a great sense of relief washed over me when I thought about how I had been able to rid the world of two Fortis men. They were two men who would never again be able to prey on Outliers. Who would never be able to harass Mira as she walked home from work, and who would never be able to hammer one more nail into the prison they were building for my people. I clung to that knowledge as I closed my eyes and my body relaxed, and it helped lull me to sleep.

After that I stopped hunting animals and started hunting men. I had always known that the further east I went the more likely I was to run into a hunting party, so every morning when I left my village, I set off in that direction. The Fortis avoided the borderland that separated the Lygan Cliffs from the wastelands, instead sticking to the valley that held the river. It was their hunting ground, their territory. And it was where I would find my next kill.

Using that knowledge to my advantage made finding the hunting parties easier than I had expected. I soon learned that they had a pattern and stuck to certain areas to hunt, making tracking them simple. They never went out on foot, and so every morning I would scour the forest in search of fresh hoof prints until I came upon a party small enough to take out. Some days, if I was feeling too tired, I would simply climb a tree and wait for them to pass by so I could shoot them from above, making it nearly impossible for anyone to get the jump on me. I never attacked unless there were three or less, but fortunately it seemed that these people liked to travel in small groups. And they never saw me coming. I was an anomaly, something that should never have existed, and it gave me the advantage.

Weeks passed and the number of deaths that followed me through the woods piled up. Two turned into five, and then twelve. With each life I took I made a notch on the belly of my bow, often running my fingers over the grooves while I sat in the trees and waited for a party to cross my path. Before long the marks went halfway up my bow, and I had to concentrate on each little groove to count them. More than fifty men had died at my hands, and despite the knowledge that my actions would most likely follow me into the afterlife. I was unable to make myself feel bad about it. The

Fortis had held me prisoner in fear for too long, but I now knew that I was stronger than my tribe had led me to believe. Stronger than anyone I knew. As long as I still had breath in my body, I would never return to the way things had been, and I would never again cower in fear.

TWENTY-THREE

S UMMER HAD COME TO AN END AND FALL WAS underway, bringing relief from the heat that radiated off the wastelands and invaded the wilds. After months of losing people, the Fortis had started sending larger hunting parties out, making it more difficult for me to find targets. But today had been a good day, and I had come across a party of two, who I had promptly killed and relieved of their game. Now though, I was exhausted from the long day of hunting and anxious to rest. Only I was forced to put the idea on hold when I returned to the village and found Mira outside the hut I still shared with my mother and sister.

"I have been waiting for you," she said when I stopped in front of her.

"I had a very busy day." I held up the rodents I had taken from the Fortis hunters.

Mira did not look at the dead animals, but instead kept her blue eyes focused on my face as she said, "Saffron asked me to talk to you."

I froze, the rodents still in the air. More than six months had gone by since my husband's death, four months since I had started hunting. The discussions that Mira and I had about the city had lessened with each passing week until she no longer brought it up at all, and the change had been a relief. She knew I had no desire to return to the city, and while I had felt obligated to listen to what was going on at first, and to make sure that Asa was still watching out for my friend, it had hurt. When she had finally stopped bringing it up, I had been relieved. I had not expected Mira to mention Sovereign City ever again, and it had never once occurred to me that Saffron would send word to me through my friend.

It could only be about one thing, but I still found myself whispering, "Why?"

"She wants you to come back to work." Mira gave me a smile that I was sure she intended to be sympathetic, but it ended up just being heartbreaking. "You always were her favorite."

"I do not know why." I finally lowered the rodents, but I was too stunned to say anything else.

Never. That was what I wanted to say. I would *never* return to Sovereign City. But I knew what saying no to this request could mean for Mira. If I disappointed Saffron, she might take it out on my friend, and based on the last reports Mira had given me about the happenings inside the walls, things were bad enough without adding to it. How could I do that to my friend? How could I add more trouble to her already burdened life?

"You can say no," Mira said as if she could read my thoughts.

"Can I? I do not want to be responsible for anyone else's pain, Mira. I already have Ronan and Bodhi's blood on my hands, I cannot add you to the list."

"You are not responsible for what happened to them," Mira said. "You are not responsible for what happens to any of us. The Sovereign make the rules and the Fortis carry them out, we are just pawns to them."

She was right, but the pain I felt over everything that had happened remained just as intense, and my worry over what else could happen remained as well.

I thought of my hours in the forest and the game I had brought back and what it meant for my family. It had helped, but not as much as the rations we used to get from Sovereign City. Then there was the medicine. My mother was fading away before my eyes, and I knew the medicine they had in the city would prolong her life, as well as ease her discomfort. How could I say no when it would help her so much?

"I need to think on it." I turned toward my hut, and Mira said nothing to try and stop me. "I will have a decision by morning."

Inside, my mother was lying in bed with fur piled up on top of her despite the warm day. My sister was nowhere in sight.

"Where is Anja?" I asked after setting the rodents on the table.

"She has been here all day looking after me. I told her to go out for a bit." When I frowned disapprovingly, my mother smiled. "She is too young to be cooped up, Indra."

"She only wants to see Jax," I said, the statement coming out angry even though I was happy that my sister was finally able to move on. I wanted her to be happy, I was just hurt and angry, and I needed someone to direct it at.

"Is that so bad? I remember you doing the same thing when you were her age."

With Bodhi.

She left it unsaid, but I knew she was thinking of my husband. He was the only boy I had ever run around with, the only one I had ever wanted to run around with, and even though it was no longer possible, that had not changed. The ache in my chest at the memory of him was less sharp than it had been, but it was still there. It probably always would be.

"That is true," I whispered as I turned back to the rodents.

My mother was quiet at first, letting me recover, and I focused on the animals in front of me, working to free them of their fur, cutting their feet off, and then preparing them to be cooked. By the time all three were done, I had relaxed a little, but my mind was still troubled. Even if my mother had not brought my dead husband up it would have been this way, because I still had a decision to make. A big one.

"What is troubling you?" she said from behind me.

"How do you know something is troubling me?" I asked, looking back at her.

My mother ran her finger over the passage markings on her forehead, and then down between her eyes. "Your skin wrinkles right here when you are thinking something through."

"I had no idea," I said.

She patted the bed at her side. "I am a good listener."

I cleaned my hands before going over to the bed. When I sat down at her side, she took my hand and gave it a reassuring squeeze. She said nothing, though. That had always been her way, quiet and patient, waiting for her girls to be ready to talk instead of trying to beat it out of us.

As usual, it worked. "Saffron sent word with Mira. She wants me to return to my position."

"That is unexpected," she said.

"Yes, it is."

My mother waited a moment to see if I was going to say more before asking, "What are you going to do?"

"I do not know."

I looked at her, really looked at her, and I could see how little time she had left. It was written in the lines of her face, in the circles under her eyes, and the loose skin that hung at her neck. My mother had always been a thin woman, but now she was skeletal. Her collarbones threatened to poke through her skin and her face was gaunt. Her skin was no longer brown but ashy from the sickness ravaging her body. Soon she would be gone from this world, but if I went back I might be able to prolong the time she had with me. If we had more food, if we once again got the medicine the Sovereign provided us with when I was working in the city, my mother could live longer.

Only, I had no desire to set foot back inside those walls. Ever.

"I am a selfish person," I said.

She laughed and shook her head. "You? No, my girl, you are anything but selfish."

"I could help more if I went back, but the thought scares me."

"Fear is normal, Indra, it is what you do with that fear that determines if you are strong or weak." She paused and gave me a weak smile. "The Head came to see me today."

My eyebrows lifted in surprise, not just at the visit, but at my mother changing the subject when we were discussing something so important. "What did he want?"

"He wanted to talk to me about you going into the woods alone to hunt. He wanted me to put a stop to it."

"But I am bringing in meat for the village. I am helping."

"You are, but he is stuck in his ways and he is afraid you will get hurt. He believes you are too weak to take care of yourself. Even if you do bring in more game than any of the men in the village."

The way her eyebrow quirked caused me to sit up straighter. She was silent for a moment, watching me, and I had the strange feeling that she knew where I was getting the game. That she knew I was killing men. That she was proud of me for it.

I looked away and swallowed. "What did you tell him?"

"I told him that you are stronger than he thinks. Stronger than anyone else in the village." She grasped my chin with her free hand and tilted my head up so I was looking her in the eye. "You are, you know. If you decide not to go into the city that is fine. We will be fine. But if you feel like this is something you need to do, either to help or to heal, you will be able to get through it. You can do it, Indra. I know it because you have the courage to go out into the woods every day even though you have always been told you should not."

"That is easy, though," I said. "In the forest it is peaceful. I do not have to look over my shoulder every second of the day, I no longer have to worry that someone will sneak up on me and if they do I can fight back." My mother's eyebrows lifted again, but I went on. "In there though, I am powerless. How can I return to that?"

"You will never be powerless, Indra. You have a strength in you that you do not see, but it is there. Bodhi saw it right away. That was why he chased you, why he took you into the woods and taught you to hunt, because he saw that you have the potential to be great. To do great things." My mother gave my hand a squeeze and then she said, "You know that you did not come from me."

I looked down at my hand in hers, at the contrasting colors of our skin. Hers as dark as fertile soil and mine tanned from my time outside, but still pale.

"It is something that does not have to be said," she continued, "but something that we should talk about while I am still alive to tell you the story."

"What story?"

"The story of how you came to be mine."

It was something I had wondered about often, but in the village it common for children to be raised by other people. Women died in childbirth, fathers met with an accident in the forest, parents got sick and children were orphaned. Our life was hard, and things happened, so I had always accepted my mother's explanation when I had asked her about my origins.

"You have always told me that my parents were unable to take care of me, so you became my parents."

"That is true," she said, "but it is not the whole truth." She took a deep breath, and then began her story. "Like my mother and her mother before her, I was working in the House of Saffron when you were born. But I had another position in the city too, one that has also been passed down, only not from mother to daughter, but to people who can be trusted. People who are strong and willing to risk their own lives. It is a position that Xandra has now taken over."

Thinking of the woman who led Bodhi into the city made my stomach turn, but it also caused my mind to spin. He had gone to her for help because she knew about the secret tunnel, and we had known about that because she had brought a baby out of the city. A baby who had been born Sovereign, but whose parents had broken the law. A baby that would now be raised as an Outlier.

"Was I born in the city?" I asked, shocked.

My mother nodded. "You were born to parents who already had a child, people who were on the one child rotation. The law said they were supposed to turn you out, which usually meant putting you outside to die. Not everyone obeys the law though, and when they need a way to get a baby out of the city, they contact a member of the underground. On the day you were born that was me, and it was also me who snuck you out of the city and brought you back here to live.

"I was not an old woman, but your father and I had been married for many years and had not yet had any children of our own. We had tried, but had failed each and every time."

Her free hand went to her face, to the passage markings on her cheekbones. She had more than anyone I knew, so many that the designs now took up most of her cheeks. Swirls and dots and lines and half circles, each of them representing a child that had not made it past her womb. "I was afraid that it might never happen for me, and when you came into my life, I felt like it was a gift from God. With no other children, the Head agreed that your father and I should keep you and raise you as our own."

Her voice faded away, but I found it impossible to utter even a word. My mind was a web of questions, none of which would come out. It had never occurred to me that I might have been born in the city, and to learn about it now, after all these years, was a shock. I was an Outlier, a member of the Winta tribe, but at the same time I was not. Not completely. I had been born Sovereign.

And who was my mother? Who in the city had defied the laws and not only given birth to me, but had sent me away so I would survive? Saffron? Was she my mother? The thought sickened me, thinking about Lysander and the things he had done not just to me, but to dozens of other women as well. Living with the memories was bad enough. If it turned out that he was actually my brother, it would make the whole thing worse. Only, I could not think about the emotionless way Saffron looked at the world and believe that she would have cared about anyone, not even her own baby, enough to defy the laws. No, it could not be her.

Still, I found that I did not care who in the city had given birth to me, because what mattered was that I was Sovereign by birth. Bodhi had been right all along: I was different. Asa too had seen this thing inside me, whatever it was, and after my husband's death I had begun to feel it too. The moment I killed that first Fortis hunter, I had allowed it to come out, the power that had been living dormant inside me for my entire life.

I thought about the Sovereign, about how they lived and the things they did, comparing it to the life I had been given, and I was suddenly more grateful than ever that the woman sitting next to me was my mother. I could have been like those people, selfish and spoiled, but I had been brought here where struggle and hard work was the only way to survive. It made no sense that I was grateful for that, but I was, because I felt as if I had been given the best of both worlds. Sovereign women were strong; I had seen it with my own eyes. Inside the walls, the women ruled. Saffron had never cowered before a man, not even the Fortis. It was something I needed to learn to emulate, to learn to be strong and unyielding to any man. But I was an Outlier too, and I knew what it meant to suffer and struggle, something no Sovereign could claim. It would take much more than what had already happened to break me, much more than anything Saffron could throw my way. I was here for a reason, thrust from luxury into poverty so I could save these people, and that was what I was going to do. How I was not yet sure, but I knew that I had the strength inside me to do it. The fact that I had been hunting the Fortis for months proved it. How many other women could say they had hunted down and killed dozens of grown men? Men more than twice their size? None that I knew of. Not even the Fortis women who worked inside the walls of the city. No, I was different, I was special, and I would return to the city and work because I was strong enough to do it. I would use my position to form a plan, because it was not enough to kill Fortis hunters when I came across them in the wilds. I needed to take the Sovereign out as well, to make sure they were not allowed to continue their reign of oppression. I would go back to work inside Sovereign City and look for cracks, and I would figure out a way to take the whole system down. Somehow.

UPRISING

Outliers Saga Book Two

Acknowledgements

The idea for *Outliers* began as a *Robin Hood* retelling, but quickly evolved into something much, much bigger. One day last fall when I wasn't feeling great, I decided to take a day off and watch *The 100* on Netflix. I'd tried watching it once a year or more before, but the first episode was so cheesy that I gave up without going any further. Since then I'd heard a lot of good things about the show, but had still been on the fence about giving it another shot until my sister-in-law, Rebekah, mentioned it to me. Thanks to her insistence that it was a show I would love, I decided to give it another chance and was immediately hooked. The world created for the show is complex and amazing, and it went a long way toward inspiring the world that I've created for this book. I wanted three different groups of people who seemed like they belonged in three different worlds even though they had been living side by side for a long time, and I wanted it to be dark and raw. *Outliers* is the result, and I think it's pretty damn amazing.

So who gets credit for helping this whole thing come together? A thank you has to go out to Netflix for making *The 100* available to me. Then there are the show's creators, who came up with an utterly amazing world, as well as a whole list of unique names that I was able to borrow from — Indra especially. Thank you also to the creators of the TV show *Outsiders* for giving me the name Asa, and *Point Break* for allowing me to think of the name Bodhi (Patrick Swayze!!). Thank you also to the members of the BOD Only Facebook group who helped me tweak my blurb when my brain felt too fried to concentrate on it.

A very special thank you goes out to my author bestie, Diana Gardin, for allowing me to borrow the term *passage markings*, which she used in her own novel, *The Lilac Sky*. When I thought about the tattoos on my characters' faces, this was the only term I could think of, and I appreciate her willingness to share it with me. But the biggest thank you of all goes out to my SIL, Rebekah, who suggested that I watch *The 100* to begin with, and who also helped me come up with the name for my city guards, the Fortis.

Jan Strohecker, thanks for being that first critical eye after I finished writing the novel, and for helping pick out any holes in the world building and plot. Thanks to my first readers and typo hunters: Courtnee McGrew, Laura Johnsen, Rebekah Caillouet, Cheer Stephenson-Papworth, and Erin Rose. Thanks also to Lori Whitwam, who answered some of my editing questions when the person I hired dropped the ball, and the BOD Authors Only group for chiming in. It's great to have a supportive community when you need some help. And last but not least, a big thank you goes out to, Amber Garcia, my PR Goddess, for setting everything up last minute.

As always, I am forced to acknowledge my husband and kids and how amazing they are. Whenever I'm really into a project they get neglected, and I appreciate not only what good sports they are, but also how supportive they are. My husband especially has no problem picking up the slack, doing laundry and running the kids to events, so I can get just a little more done, and I couldn't ask for a better support system!

About the Author

Kate L. Mary is an award-winning author of New Adult and Young Adult fiction, ranging from Post-apocalyptic tales of the undead, to Speculative Fiction and Contemporary Romance. Her Young Adult book, *When We Were Human*, was a 2015 Moonbeam Children's Book Awards Silver Medal winner for Young Adult Fantasy/Sci-Fi Fiction, and a 2016 Readers' Favorite Gold Medal winner for Young Adult Science Fiction. Don't miss out on the *Broken World* series, an Amazon bestseller and fan favorite.

For more information about Kate, check out her website: www.KateLMary.com

Made in the USA
Coppell, TX
20 February 2022